Bought and Paid For

Bought and Paid For

A Jan Phillips Novel

Michael Halfhill

iUniverse, Inc.

New York Lincoln Shanghai

Bought and Paid For
A Jan Phillips Novel

All Rights Reserved © 2004 by Michael Halfhill

iUniverse, Inc.

For information address:
iUniverse, Inc.
2021 Pine Lake Road, Suite 100
Lincoln, NE 68512
www.iuniverse.com

Bought and Paid For is a work of fiction. Names, characters, places, and incidents are the product of the author's imagination or are used fictitiously Any resemblance to actual persons, living or dead, events or locales is entirely coincidental. Illegal acts depicted here are strongly condemned by the author.

ISBN: 0-595-30490-7

Printed in the United States of America

To Peter with love.

Acknowledgements

This book would not have been possible with out the support of so many.

Peter for his patience, long hours of work and support.

Francine, Lyndon and Mary for reading my story.

The "Admiral" who read it first and encouraged me to keep going.

And special thanks to Antonio Marquez who pointed me in the right direction and shared the experience of publishing a first book.

CHAPTER 1

▼

Jan Phillips sat with Bobby O'Farrell one late afternoon as the two watched the latest episode of *The Sopranos*. Bobby's dad worked for the local cable company and their household was the only one in their run-down neighborhood to have expanded programming like HBO and Showtime. It was one of the perks his dad had in lieu of a decent wage for risking life and limb dragging miles of TV cable over steep city roofs. Jan and Bobby sat and watched the cast credits roll across the screen.

"Well I gotta go," Jan said with a sigh.

"Wait, I have something to show you."

"Okay, but make it quick. My mom'll be home in a couple of hours and I gotta get some work done before she gets in."

"Okay, okay." Bobby said. "Keep your shirt on. I'll be right back."

Jan looked around the "basement den", as Bobby's dad called it. The overstuffed couch had that same musty smell every other couch in every basement family room in every row house in Kensington had. Dotted Swiss fabric covered the three tiny windows that were wholly inadequate in providing light or fresh air. A ratty sheep skin rug sprawled across the cracked concrete floor.

Jack O'Farrell's trophies and ribbons, earned when he was a high school jock, ringed the basement walls on homemade shelves. They were the only items kept dusted and polished.

Bobby returned with the newest edition of *Xbox Speed Kings*.

"Geeze Bobby! Where did you get that?" Jan gasped with envy.

"Whattya think? I bought it," Bobby said.

"You bought it? Did you get a job or something?" Jan asked.

"Well, kinda but you gotta promise you won't say nothin'. Okay?"

"What are you talking about?" When Bobby hesitated, Jan said, "Look, you're my best friend. If you don't want me to say anything, I won't."

"I got it in Center City, on Van Wyck Street."

Jan looked puzzled. "Van Wyck? There's nothing up there but big houses and apartment buildings. I didn't know there was a game store there. Is it some over-stock outlet place?"

"Uh, you really don't know, do you?"

"Know what?" Jan said. "What's to know?"

"Jan, guys make big money at Fifteenth and Van Wyck. All's you have to do is let queers…, you know, do it to you."

"Do what?"

"Oh come on Jan! You know—suck your dick."

Bobby pulled four twenty-dollar bills from the pocket on the side of his baggy pant leg.

"Look at this!"

Jan stared at the money in Bobby's hand. "Is this a joke? What are you talking about? Are you queer or something?"

"Or something Jan. I'm not queer. I just do it for the money. Look why don't you go up with me this Friday and I can show you?"

Jan's hand flew out, grabbing Bobby by his hair. "To do what! You filthy faggot! Don't you ever say a think like that to me again!"

Bobby pulled out of Jan's grip. "Hey take it easy! I was just trying to share the wealth. You don't have to freak out on me. I just thought you might want to make some easy money. I bet those old geezers would really go for you in a big way. With your hair you could pass for younger than you are and they like 'em young. Ha ha ha ha," Bobby laughed.

Tears started to stream down Jan's cheeks. "Fuck you! Why did you have to screw everything up, Bobby? You were my best friend! But now…." Shaking his head, Jan backed away, turned, and ran up the stairs, out the back door and down the alley. Jan wanted to be alone. He *needed* to be alone.

$$*\qquad*\qquad*\qquad*$$

The following day, Jan avoided everyone in the neighborhood, especially Bobby O'Farrell. He spent most of his time checking on the job applications he had in the small businesses that struggled to stay afloat in this economically depressed area of the city. Nothing.

Wandering into Minqua Park he found it deserted, except for two old black men playing chess in the shade of a honey locust tree. Jan chose a picnic table nearby and lay on his back. He looked up and imagined the faces of Olympian gods from the lazy clouds that passed in the late summer sky.

He began thinking about the things that he'd change in his life if he could. His name was first on the list. Jan hated his name. It was a girl's name. He begged his mom to call him by Christopher, his middle name, but her reply was always the same: "There's nothing wrong with it. Your name is a good Dutch name. Your grandfather and great grandfather were called Jan and they were rough and tough stevedores at the Port of Philadelphia. Our heritage can be traced back to the first settlers who helped William Penn found Philadelphia."

"Well," thought Jan. "If you happen to be a rough and tough stevedore you could be called Pricilla and get away with it."

In the six years he had attended Saint Dominic's Academy, Father Sobinski had pushed him through an academic program reserved for college-bound kids where families had the money that Jan's family didn't. Jan often wondered just what the priest intended. If he had an agenda he never discussed it with him. Without the money to continue his schooling, the college prep courses were more of a liability than an asset when it came to finding the kinds of jobs offered to a newly graduated high school kid. With his father dead and his mother working a minimum wage job, Jan knew there would be no college for him unless he went into the seminary or into the army. Both were options that were equally unacceptable to him. Furthermore, Father Sobinski had been transferred to Rome and with him went Jan's only source of direction, as well as the financial shield that allowed him, along with his sisters and brother to attend Saint Dom's. So what was the point?

Jan focused his eyes on another cloud. This time a wispy figure lashed a horse drawn chariot into the sun. He began to think about what happened at Bobby's yesterday.

"Jan?"

Startled, Jan sat up and saw his mother approaching.

"Mom! What are you doing here?"

Jan's mother Joy, stood by the picnic table. Her hair, once blond and lustrous like Jan's, was streaked with gray. It hung around a lined face that was considered pretty by the neighborhood boys who pursued her when she was Jan's age.

Jan remembered when she came to his eighth grade graduation Mass. She wore makeup and a new dress. He thought she looked pretty then, but that was then.

She sat next to him on the table, looked away, then took a deep breath and spoke to him, "Jan, I have to be straight with you. You've got to leave home and start on your own. You've wasted all summer when you could have been working and helping me with the bills. I just can't afford to take care of you and your sisters and brother anymore. You're eighteen; you're a man now. It's time for you to go."

"What are you talking about? Out on my own? Wasted the summer! Sobinski made me study night and day *and weekends* all summer long so I could graduate before he left for Rome. I've got job applications out all over Kensington! I'm trying! It's not my fault I can't find a job! Why do I have to leave?" he said defensively.

Jan's mother set her jaw and looked him in the eye. "I can't afford you kids anymore!"

Jan chewed his lower lip to keep from crying. "How about Aunt Susan. Can I go stay with her?"

"Oh, Jan, grow up! Your Aunt Sue didn't even want her own son! You know that's why Daniel lives with us so get real!"

"This isn't fair. I'll try harder."

"Fair? You wanna talk about fair? Look at *me*. Look at *my* life and then we'll talk about what's fair! You gotta month, then you gotta go if I have to drag you out by the hair. So get off your ass and get moving!"

Jan's mother stood, turned on her heel she stormed out of the park.

Jan sat stunned. His mom had never talked to him like this before. What was he going to do? He wondered what he had done to deserve this. He tried to be a good son. He got good grades in school and unlike some of the neighbor's kids, he was never in trouble with the law. He had no idea she was thinking about getting rid of him. Where would he go? How would he live? He didn't know anybody who would take him in. How could he survive without money? Could he survive on the street?

Bobby's words about making money letting old men do it to him crept into the back of Jan's mind. It did look like Bobby made a lot of money from it. Would it be enough? He thought about what he would have to do to get that money; cold wrinkled hands groping him; boozy mouths full of rotting teeth breathing on him; the smell of body odor in his nose—the kind of old men he'd see sitting in the park all day drinking from their brown paper bags—touching him for money! Maybe if he closed his eyes it wouldn't be so bad. He wouldn't have to pretend he liked it. If he did do it, it would only be as a last resort. Disgusted, he tried to drive those thoughts away.

CHAPTER 2

▼

One month to the day, Jan gazed at his reflection in an antique shop window on Van Wyck Street. No doubt about it, he looked far younger than eighteen. He wasn't as tall as guys he went to school with; they all had shot up to respectable heights while Jan remained locked at five feet seven. Unlike the others, he hadn't sprouted any facial hair to pronounce him a man. While acne ravaged their faces, generous genes blessed him with an unblemished face. Like Bobby had said, cool, gray eyes, golden hair, and sweet looks combined with a genuine innocence made Jan a natural to be singled-out by the chicken hawks that frequented the city. That he hadn't been approached for sex in the city so far, was a minor miracle—but then again he rarely ventured into Center City and certainly never alone—until now.... A whole month had passed and he still hadn't found a way to survive on his own.

The idea of sex for money still nauseated him. The more he considered the prospect of sex with a man the more uncomfortable he started to feel. So why did his mind wander back to the subject? He wasn't gay: he didn't think about guys that way. He had never had sex with another person. He wasn't even sure how to do it. Most of the guys he knew had already lost their virginity, at least that's what they said. He never seemed to have the time or opportunity to meet anyone to even be interested in. He never talked with "the guys" about sex—that seemed too dirty. His whole life was taken up with his family, homework, and the priests and nuns at Saint Dominic's Academy. Sure, like all young guys he jerked-off, but afterwards he always felt guilty. Didn't Father Sobinski say he was killing potential babies that God wanted for his own? Jan prayed that Jesus would forgive him, and he tried hard not to do it again. Sometimes he avoided the temptation; often he didn't. But for all that praying, now he was preparing to sell himself for sex. What would Jesus think of that!

Still, the idea of the money nagged at him. Jan had to leave home and soon.

"I'm not a fag. I won't have to *do* anything, and no one will know if I do," he told himself.

It was the last Sunday in September. The air was cool but Jan was sweating. He was just one block from the "tenderloin district." He had made this same trek alone into Center City twice before, but both times he wimped-out. Both times fear and inexperience made up equal parts in a recipe for failure. Each time he panicked after standing around for a half hour. People passed by without even looking at him. He was uncertain if he was supposed to say or do something to attract attention.

"The third time is supposed to be the charm..., right?" he asked himself. Again, he wasn't sure if he could go through with it. The bus returning to Kensington would be arriving soon.

CHAPTER 3

▼

Tim Morris loved the "Mary-Go-Round", the one square block of Center City streets from Fifteenth along Van Wyck to Sixteenth then left to Dyke and left again to Fifteenth and back up to Van Wyck. Local and out-of-state cars cruised the block all night. It was a happy coincidence that all these streets were marked one-way, making it all the easier for solicitation; boys and young men could walk in a direction against the traffic to see and be seen. Business was always brisk. If you wanted "free sex", you had to drive six blocks further on to Trenton Place. The hawks were older there and so were the chickens—much older.

Tim also loved his Thirteenth floor apartment in the old Saint Roi building on Van Wyck Street. The largest of all the units, it boasted enormous floor to ceiling windows that gave a wide view of the Mary-Go-Round.

Tim had a weakness for young guys, and this location provided him with ample company on nights when he wasn't working late at his law firm, The Templars of Law. Tim was averse to paying for sex, however he often found that many of the "street merchants" were willing to share a bed for a shared meal, especially on a snowy night when business was off.

This afternoon he was sitting in a leather club chair with his binoculars trained on the street when he noticed *that* kid again. After seeing him twice before, both times on Sundays, Tim had christened him "GL", for Goldie Locks.

He wondered about this boy. His behavior was all wrong for a hustler, and he seemed ill at ease, almost as if he were lost though he didn't seem to be. GL didn't look directly at the cars as they passed but then again he always ducked into the corner flower shop when a cop car came into view. And what about this daylight routine? And only on Sundays? Chicken hawks didn't fly before night-fall, and rarely on a Sunday afternoon after being out late on Saturday night.

Could it be that this youngster was out for the first time? Tim turned the questions over in his mind as he raised the binoculars again. The bus from Kensington to Center City had just pulled from the curb. GL was gone.

CHAPTER 4

▼

Three weeks after spotting Goldie Locks, Tim still was no closer to discovering any more about him aside from what he had already deduced. The Kensington bus passes through two other barren neighborhoods before arriving in the heart of the city; GL could be from any of these. It wasn't much to go on. He put the idea of asking the regulars who hustled across the street from the Saint Roi out of his mind because none of them were out scoring men at five o'clock in the afternoon; they wouldn't have seen GL.

As far as Tim could see there were only four possibilities here. Goldie Locks would eventually score and lose his presumed innocence; be picked up by cops and hauled off to a city lock-up where he would most definitely be corrupted or return home and become a barber never to be seen again; or Tim just might get the opportunity to pass on to this kid the chance of a lifetime—and *redeem* himself, if that was possible.

On this last Sunday in September, low clouds pushed along by a damp wind confirmed the forecaster's prediction of an early fall storm. Tim walked briskly up Van Wyck Street. With just two blocks to go, the sky split like a cloudy glacier. Globs of water clipped concrete windowsills set high above the street making a fine mist that mixed with the heavy downpour. He was grateful that Mrs. Santos, his housekeeper, had insisted he take a waterproof jacket.

"*Señor* Tim, the weather man said it was going to be a dry day. You know what that means. Rain! Take the jacket," she insisted.

A woman dragging a reluctant toy poodle shouldered a path through the crowd of people and dashed for cover. She gave Tim a look that spoke volumes when he made contact as he passed the doorway she cowered in, "Don't even think about it, Bub! This is my spot!"

Icy needles jabbed his face as he jogged along the irregular brick sidewalk, head down, trying to miss the deepening puddles. He wasn't looking when the Kensington bus swung off Broad Street on to Van Wyck sliding to a stop just a few feet from him. The whoosh of opening doors made Tim turn; there was Goldie Locks. Both made a dash to the flower shop a few feet away. They shivered in their soaked clothing.

Tim laughed. "Well, we almost made it!"

Jan looked down at his clothes. "Wow, I'm wet clear through…it feels cold in here."

Grabbing a twenty-dollar bunch of flowers, Tim paid the clerk and turned to Jan. "I live just across the street. Want to help me put these in water? You can dry off too."

Jan snapped back. This was the city, not Saint Dom's parish hall. This was a stranger, not someone's mother setting up at a church dinner; but the man seemed pleasant enough and didn't try to hide the invitation by lowering his voice.

"Money for sex". Jan had repeated the mantra all the way into the city. So what was he doing, running off to some guy's apartment just to get dry? This wasn't going to put cash in his pocket.

Still, he was wet and cold. Jan stammered, "Yeah, okay I guess…Thanks. I need to get dry before my bus comes along and I won't get dry in here."

"My name's Tim. What's yours?"

"Jan. Jan Phillips," he replied loudly enough for the clerk to hear. It was the kind of self-preserving act kids learn early in the city.

As they stood under the red and white awning, Jan took **a** good look at Tim for the first time. He regarded him with curiosity rather than suspicion, not knowing what to make of this guy. He certainly didn't look like the kind of man he had expected to offer money for sex. In fact he looked like he could be a model, about six feet tall, with curly dark hair streaked with highlights, strong features and an easy-going smile. Jan figured him to be thirty-six, maybe thirty-eight years old.

A lull in traffic allowed them to race across Van Wyck Street, dodging cars and puddles. Success was limited. Tim's pant legs were soaked while Jan's canvas sneakers sounded as if he were walking on sponges.

The Saint Roi's lobby was awash in soft lights shining from recessed bulbs fifteen feet above the glassy marble floor.

"Gee! This looks like a church!" Jan blurted before he realized he sounded like a dope.

Tim thought a moment. "It does, kind of. Wait until you see my place. It's definitely not a church."

The desk attendants knew Tim had an odd assortment of visitors and took no notice as he ushered Jan into the elevator. Moments later the elevator deposited them at his floor. Waiting for a reaction, Tim stood aside as they entered his apartment.

Jan stood back and looked at what he thought heaven must be like if it were an apartment. His notion of heaven was about to change. He glanced at Tim for re-assurance as he stepped inside.

CHAPTER 5

▼

The Saint Roi, built in the early 1900s, was twenty stories high and filled half a city block. The architect designed all the units above the tenth floor in penthouse luxury. Only two units occupied any one floor, and Tim claimed both on the thirteenth. Parquet floors gleaming from decades of hand polishing and twelve foot ceilings gave the feeling of rooms soaring into space. Sectional sofas in white damask reflected off walls covered in tan leather. Soft light drizzled through porcelain grills high above them. The outside walls had floor to ceiling windows presenting a wall of glass. The ninety-seven-story Penn Central Towers, seven blocks away, looked so close, Jan felt like he could reach out and touch them.

Tim had felt much the same way when he first saw this place fifteen years before. It seemed like a million years ago. Peter de Main, the man who lived here then had been the only person who had ever offered him the kind of love and protection he craved.

Tim walked into the kitchen carrying the flowers.

"There are some towels in the spare bathroom down the hall. It's the last door on the right. There's a washer/dryer stack unit in there too. You can dry your things and then join me in the living room. All I need are dry pants," he said as he pulled out a ceramic vase for the flowers.

"What did you say your name is?" he called out from behind a center isle workstation.

Jan moved passed the kitchen door and he pulled off his Polo shirt.

"Jan," he replied.

Looking up from the flowers, Tim caught sight of Jan. Their eyes met for a second as his semi-nude figure passed by.

"Jan, eh? Nice name."

"It sucks. Unless you like having a girl's name," Jan answered.

"It's better than Goldie Locks. That's what I named you when I first began watching you from my window."

Silence.

"Goldie Locks?" Jan said in a quieter, less friendly tone. "What? You were watching me...? Why?"

"Go get dry and we'll talk," Tim ordered.

While Jan stripped in the bathroom, Tim went into the master bedroom suite and slipped out of his damp clothes and into a pair of soft jeans and a cashmere sweater.

Swathed in an oversized terry bath sheet, Jan returned to the living room where Tim sat in his leather club chair with binoculars trained on the street. He stood quietly looking over Tim's shoulder. Tim put the binoculars on a side table and smiled up at him.

"This was all I could find. My underwear wasn't all that wet so I left them on. This thing is awfully big. Is it okay?" Jan said.

Tim's smile broadened. "Yes of course. It's made to be extra large."

Jan wrinkled his forehead. "You didn't answer—why were you watching me?"

Tim got right to the point. "You're hustling and I think you're new on the street. That's why I was watching you...and I want to have sex with you before anybody else gets into your pants. Oh, and you're not a very good hustler. Now, tell me I'm wrong."

Jan couldn't believe his ears. This guy wasn't old and wrinkly. He was movie star handsome. "He can't be queer!" he thought.

Jan blurted, "No! I'm not. I...Well, I don't...I haven't...Oh, damn!"

Jan's hands covered his face, trying to hide his confusion.

Tim reached out, grabbing the towel and Jan's briefs underneath. Jan twisted aside just as Tim tugged at the fabric. The towel fell away, leaving Jan with his briefs pulled down far enough to expose his smooth shaven privates.

"How many guys your age shave their crotches? If you're not a hustler, why do you shave your pubic hair?" Tim sneered.

In the mean time Jan had hurriedly covered himself. His face burned red.

"I heard that old men pay a lot of money if they think they're getting it on with someone younger. That's why!" Jan answered.

"So you *are* a hustler!"

"No!" cried Jan.

"Okay," Tim said, his patience running thin. "It's time to fess up. What are you up to? Oh and by the way, most older men have been around long enough that they know a shaved crotch when they feel one, so you won't be fooling anybody." Not knowing what else to do, Jan slumped to the soft, deep-pile carpet.

CHAPTER 6

▼

Jan pulled the terry towel across his lap. He sat with his head bent so that his chin rested on his chest; blond hair hung down each side of his face hiding his trembling frown. He wasn't sure he could explain the reasons that brought him to the point of being nearly naked in a stranger's home.

"What do you want from me," he said.

Tim sighed. "Okay. Once more, what's going on with you?"

Jan shook his head from side to side as if that act would throw off his dilemma. Finally, he began in a small, barely audible voice. "I'm alone."

When Tim didn't respond, Jan looked up to see if he was listening. Tim just smiled and nodded.

"I'm going to be alone in a few days. I just turned eighteen," Jan added.

Tim's hand shot out taking the teen's chin in a firm grip. He turned Jan's face studying the pale, smooth skin, looking deep and hard trying to determine if Jan was telling a lie. Was it possible for an eighteen year old to look as if he were sixteen?

Jan looked back without emotion.

Releasing his hold Tim said, "Go on…."

Jan's discussion with his mother, about his future or lack of one, had been the hardest he had ever gone through, talking about it now to a stranger seemed just as hard somehow.

Jan sighed. "In a few days I have to leave home and be on my own. My mom talked to me about not being able to support me and my sisters and brother—I'm the oldest. I looked for a job and I can't find one, so I don't bring in money. She just doesn't make enough for five kids and now she says I'm not a kid anymore."

Jan gulped for air and continued, "It's not that she hates me or anything like that but I'm no good if I don't pull my weight."

Tim thought, "This sounds like a bad novel...."

"What about your father?" he asked.

Jan shook his head. "My dad died six years ago. Maybe you read about it. He was the man who got crushed to death at the Navy Yard. It was in all the papers."

Tim remembered the incident. A contractor was painting the dockside of a battleship when he fell between the ship and the pier.

"What about insurance? There must have been a big payout. What happened to that money?"

Jan rubbed his forehead. "There wasn't any insurance because it wasn't an accident. My dad killed himself and the insurance people said they wouldn't cover suicide. Can you imagine being so unhappy that you would get yourself mushed to death?"

"If it was suicide, why did the papers say it was an accident?"

Jan sighed. "Father Sobinski, he was the dean at Saint Dominic's Academy. He and my dad were best friends in school. Sobinski was a big shot for the Cardinal here in Philly so he got the coroner to make the report look like it could have been an accident so when the papers got the story we all wouldn't have to be embarrassed. He couldn't do anything about the money but he was able to get me into Saint Dominic's Academy without mom having to pay. Now he's been transferred to Rome so my sisters and brother will have to go to public school."

Trying to find a bright spot in this miserable tale, Tim said, "Well at least you got a good education. I hear Saint Dom's is a good school."

Jan laughed for the first time. "A good school! It hasn't gotten me anywhere! So what if I can say, 'Would you like fries with that sir?' in Latin. No one's hiring teenage scholars at McDonalds."

Jan looked away. "Besides I'm a so-so student. Just B's and a coupla A's. The only thing I have to offer is between my legs. Do you know what that feels like?"

"I can guess," said Tim.

Tim got up and headed toward the kitchen. Turning, he looked down at Jan. "I'm thirsty. Would you like a Coke or ginger ale? I don't have any beer, and I won't offer you anything from the bar."

"Coke is fine. I don't drink alcohol. I don't like the taste," Jan answered.

"Then don't drink it. If you drink booze for any reason other than the taste you're drinking for the wrong reason," Tim said.

Advice from a stranger at a time like this. Jan still wasn't sure what this guy wanted but he was feeling more comfortable with Tim. He almost forgot he was naked under the towel.

Tim returned with Cokes and handed one to Jan. "Tell me about your family."

Jan took a sip. It wouldn't hurt to just talk to this guy some more would it?

"There's my mom. Then there's Sara and Paula, they're twins. They'll be fifteen in December. Then there's my brother Daniel, he's fourteen, he's actually not my brother. He's adopted from my mom's sister. His parents are real assholes and didn't want a kid, so my mom and dad got him. The last is my baby sister Ruth. We live in a row house in Kensington. Mom had to take some kind of house loan so we could be okay with money for a while but it went fast."

"It's called a home equity loan," Tim interjected. "It means that the bank subtracted the difference from what the house is worth today from what is still owed on the mortgage. Then they loaned your mom eighty percent of that amount. Usually it isn't much in homes in that section of the city."

Jan gave Tim a wondering look and sniffed, "How do you know so much about that section of the city? I can't see you driving out there for picnics or shopping."

Tim laughed. Roaming that bleak neighborhood, which could be as hot as the Devil's anvil in summer heat and gray and rundown and depressing in every other season, was not something he would ordinarily do.

"Let's just say I know a thing or two about this city. How much did your mom get from the bank?"

Jan thought a moment. "I think she said three thousand dollars."

Tim squatted in front of Jan. "Did you really think you could make up that amount by selling your ass?"

Jan stiffened. "My ass! All I was going to do was let old men suck my dick. I didn't say anything about my ass!"

Tim looked at him. "First of all, when you're in some guy's car out in the reeds behind the airport, miles from home, you don't get a say in what you will or won't do. Second, the going rate for sex with these guys ranges from thirty to forty dollars a pop, *and* if you're real lucky old Judge Harkness will pay you seventy-five bucks to let him watch his chauffer fuck you. That's the reality of your chosen profession. To earn, let's say, three thousand at a rate of, oh, let's be generous, forty bucks a trick, you'll have to be out there seventy-five Sundays in a row, rain, snow or shine.

"Oh," Tim added. "And don't forget about the other guys on the street. They'll be waiting for you to get back from your suck sessions with their hands out for a share. I should warn you that they can be very persuasive when they demand a portion of your hard earned dollars—no pun intended. And believe me, you'll earn every penny."

Jan's eyes bulged in disbelief. He pulled back as if he had just noticed Tim growing another head.

The pair sat in silence for a while.

Finally, Tim said, "Did you honestly think you could survive on the street? It gets freezing cold out there. What kind of mother just says get out?"

"I think she thinks that someone will come to the rescue. You know like the church or something. I'm eighteen so I'm supposed to be a grown up and everything will work out somehow."

Tim shook his head. Abandoned, shoved out of the nest, shunned, no matter how you slice it boys and girls face this crisis everyday. Tim knew all too well the consequences of life without a family. They sat in silence again. Tim began to formulate his redemption in his head.

"I have an idea. What's your home phone number?"

Jan looked out the window at the dismal sky. "Why?"

"I want to speak with your mom. I have a proposal, a quid pro quo," Tim said.

"A quid pro quo? What do you mean?"

Tim looked into Jan's eyes and hoped he would understand and agree.

"Your mother needs money and she has you, I have money and I *want* you. It would be a simple exchange. She gives me you with no future interference and I give her four thousand, an extra thousand for the interest she would pay the bank."

"What?" Jan couldn't believe his ears. "You can't buy people!"

As soon as he had spoken, Jan instinctively drew back as if to ward off a slap. He had learned in Catholic school that sass would get you a red ear.

Tim gave a wry smile. "Jan, with enough money you can buy power, sex, murder, mayhem and especially girls and boys. So, do you think she'll go for it?"

Jan's mind was in a whirl. Tim was eager but it didn't look like he was a psycho or something. He was serious…Jan had never heard of anything like this, let alone considered it could happen to him. Would it be a bad thing? This guy was good looking, lived in a nice place, he seemed okay.

And then, almost without knowing what he was saying, "She might, if I ask her, but what if *I* won't go for it? What would I have to do?"

Tim walked to Jan, lifted him from the floor and gave him his first kiss. Jan was as rigid as a board. It had never occurred to him that guys kissed one another. He relaxed just enough for Tim to slip his tongue into his mouth. The kiss was long, wet and very hot. The towel fell from Jan's hips. He wanted to reach for it but Tim's grip was too strong to break.

When they finally parted, Jan put his head on Tim's shoulder. He let himself go to a rush of feelings—good, warm, hopeful feeling—butterflies in his stomach and a familiar but no longer shameful tightening in his loins. Jan had been taught all his life that this was wrong and that he would be damned for being queer. He also knew he couldn't—or rather wouldn't—leave.

"Whoa...." he said to himself.

An involuntary tear rolled down his cheek.

CHAPTER 7

▼

Tim held Jan in his arms for a long time, swaying to the rhythms of their heart-beats; savoring the feel of Jan's skin, with all the muscle tone of youth aching, eager to be pleased. He felt as if this could be something good for both of them.

A stray beam of sunlight pierced the gloomy sky and reflected in a wall-sized mirror lighting the room with unexpected brilliance. Jan looked at the mirror and saw himself in Tim's arms.

Tim looked and saw not Jan, but Peter de Main holding him that first time so long ago. It was if Peter was saying, *Tim, this is the one.* Tim blinked. The mirage was gone.

Tim let go and stepped away. "You'd better get dressed. Your bus will be here soon."

Jan was confused. His new roaring erection begged for pleasure, but his mind was relieved to be free of the situation for now.

"Don't you want me? What's going to happen now…What am I supposed to do?" Jan said.

"You go home and talk with your mom about this. You don't have to go into the sex thing if you don't want to. Just say that I got wind of the situation and have a deal she may be willing to consider. If she's up for it, then we'll meet tomorrow. If not, then I guess I'll be watching you down on the street from up here."

Tim knew this was a gamble with high stakes but thought it was worth it. It was also emotional blackmail, and on a susceptible youngster at that.

"What's you mother's name?"

Jan's eyes wandered around the room taking it all in.

He sighed. "Joy Phillips." Suddenly he came back to his senses. "You still haven't answered me. What if *I* won't go for your deal?"

Tim answered quickly. "You've just laid out the situation for yourself. Now, *you* tell me your options. Do you have a better offer?"

Jan admitted to himself that he didn't.

Tim knew his answer.

Jan wrapped the towel around his waist in belated modesty and walked down the hall to the bathroom to retrieve his clothes from the dryer.

Tim was looking down on Van Wyck Street when Jan came up behind him.

"Wait a minute!" Jan said. "I'm eighteen! Why does my mom have to know anything about this?"

Tim smiled. "Not just a pretty face after all! Look, I want to help you out, but the most important thing in life you'll ever learn is that everything can be had for money and that nothing, absolutely nothing in this life is free. I want your mother to be out of your life because my life has no place for the kinds of complications parents can make in a situation like this. And not to put too fine a point on it, I want you now not at some future date. This is a contract—a job if you like…not a relationship. It's as simple as that."

Jan was confused again. Hadn't he felt something when they embraced? Some electricity?

"Trust me," Tim said. "Nothing in your life has prepared you for this kind of adventure. I, on the other hand, have experienced something like it before."

Jan thought about the money and what Tim had said about life on the streets. He didn't know if Tim was telling the truth about that or if he was just trying to scare him. One thing was for sure, he was very scared.

"What a mess," he sighed. He looked Tim in the eye and said, "Okay, I'll ask her about it tonight."

There, he had done it. He had committed himself to an arrangement he had no control over, with no idea how or where it go.

A clap of thunder greeted them as they walked through the polished bronze doors of the Saint Roi. Jan and Tim both wondered if it was an omen of things to come.

Jan sprinted across the street to the bus stop. The wheezing coach lumbered to the curb moments later. Boarding, he took a window seat, smiled at Tim and nodded his complicity once more before the bus eased back into traffic.

CHAPTER 8

▼

Jan rehearsed his story on the hour long ride back home. The massive skyscrapers gave way to block after block of faded red brick row houses until he arrived back in Kensington, a flat, treeless square mile of sameness. Jan had lived his whole life in the confines of this brick neighborhood with its noisy elevated train, boarded windows of long abandoned businesses and ankle deep trash. Their row house, a three story, was one room wide and two rooms deep. A crooked sycamore tree darkened the front of the building. For the last five years he had attempted to be the man in the family with no authority and no money to see the job was done well. Now he was asked to leave, like an unwanted guest at a birthday party. Stung and resentful Jan felt more alone than ever.

He walked into the living room as his mother sat down to watch the early Channel Ten News. The contrast between this dingy room and the splendid one he had left not more than two hours before struck Jan like a punch in the gut. He had always accepted the parlor and all the other worn out rooms in the small row house as his whole world. It never occurred to him that any other kind of life could exist. He sensed the potential for something different—something better for he first time in his life. He didn't quite understand it and it frightened him too but he wanted it. He wanted it very much.

Joy looked more tired than usual today. He hesitated bringing the subject up to his mom when she seemed so beaten down. It was cool in the house but Jan was sweating again. The butterflies in his stomach hatched, mated and died with every breath he took but he knew it was now or never. His brother and sisters would be home soon, and he didn't want them to hear the screaming he was sure would follow once he told her about Tim and his proposal. Jan sat next to his mother, reached over and held her hand.

Without searching for more courage, he said, "Mom, I need to talk about what you said…about my having to move out…I mean."

Joy switched off the TV.

"Okay," she said simply.

Slowly, Jan picked carefully through the day's events like a knotted thread being pulled from a spool and untangled.

Joy's eyes widened in disbelief.

Finally, she cried, "Is this some kind of joke? I've never heard of such a thing! What have you been up to while I'm at work?"

Jan backed away, not sure if he was going to get a swat.

"This is no joke," he said. "The truth is, this is my chance to get out of a no-win situation."

"So you're a fag? You think you're a fag? Where did that come from?"

Jan really didn't know if he was really gay but he had to admit that what Tim did to him felt good at the time.

"What I am isn't the point. Will you meet him or not?"

"You're God damned right I'll meet with this perv!" she shouted.

Jan had seen his mom angry before, but never like this. Just then, the kitchen door slammed. Jan put a finger to his mouth shushing his mother in mid-sentence. His brother and sisters were home with their usual noise and chatter.

"We're in the parlor," Jan called out.

Jan's four siblings burst into the room, each yelling to be heard over the other.

"Hold it!" Joy said. "What's going on? What's got you all riled up?"

"Mr. and Mrs. Kennedy want to know if we, I mean all us kids, can go with them to Saint Dom's for the Polish Festival!" Sara announced.

"Can we, mom? Pleeeeaze, pleeeeaze, pleeeeaze," they all chimed at once.

"We won't be any trouble. We promise."

"What about your homework?"

"All done," they said in unison.

Joy considered their hopeful faces. "Yes, you can go, but I want no wildness now. Do you hear me? The Kennedys are not as young as you all. I don't want them worn out on account of you all being crazy. Paula, I want you to keep an eye on Ruth. Sara did it the last time you all went out, so it's your turn."

Paula readily agreed. For a chance to go to the festival and flirt with the boys from Cardinal Dougherty High she would have consented to do anything.

"C'mon, Jan," Daniel said, tugging on his brother's arm. "They have the car outside right now!"

"You guys go ahead. Mom and I've got some things we need to talk about."

The screen door slammed with an ear splitting bang as the children dashed out to the Kennedy's car. Joy went to the door to wave them all a goodbye, then turned and started with Jan again.

"Have you said any of this queer stuff to Father Sobinski?"

"No. Not yet," Jan answered quietly.

"Well I can imagine what he'd say! Half the church is queer. Well, what can you expect from men who wear black dresses to work? What I want to know is, why? Why sex for money? I didn't raise you like that!"

"Money! Because you told me I had to get a job or get out and—"

"Hold it right there, Mister!" Joy cut in. "Nobody said you had to be a whore! I said get a job or move out because I can't make it with only my minimum wage job. Did you know that I tried to get us food stamps? They said I made too much money to qualify! Imagine, even with all you kids at home, I make too much money! So don't try to put your bad choices on me!"

Joy was tired; more than tired, she was used up and still just thirty-seven. She had been making babies, satisfying a sexually demanding husband and working at the Broadway Market in Kensington most her adult life. After Jan's father died, she had borrowed money all over town to keep her children in food and clothes and buy some extras at Christmas.

Finally, she had turned to Father Sobinski for guidance, hoping that he could suggest a service the church could provide. Fat chance! All he told her was that she had to be firm with Jan and get him pulling his weight.

Sobinski, she knew, had entered seminary at age fifteen. From that time on, he had been cosseted in the priesthood, never really being hungry, never having to wear mended clothes or shoes with holes, never having to pay for a car or a utility bill. What the fuck did he know about need? Passing out turkey dinners on Thanksgiving and comforting homeless people with pats on the head once a year may get him a crown in heaven, but it didn't do a damn thing to solve her problems.

Jan was getting angry himself.

"I'm not asking you to be responsible for my choices! But really, what choices have I had with you riding herd on me? With Sobinski and Sister Mary Frivolous at Saint Dom's on my ass all day, the only choice I've been allowed to make, right or wrong, is whether to use an active or passive verb in a Latin text!" he yelled.

The two of them talked back and forth and around in circles. After a while, they moved into the kitchen. Like she always did when she was avoiding facing the unpleasant, Joy busied herself. While she wiped the enamel-topped table that took up much of the floor space in the tiny room, Jan kept a safe distance at the opposite side. He didn't need a black eye to add to his troubles, but he wasn't about to let this go either.

"You just haven't tried to find work," Joy said without looking up.

"The hell I haven't! My application is in every store on Christopher Columbus Boulevard!" Jan said defensively. "Did I tell you that I applied at Staples? They told me that they would be hiring soon and I'd get a call. Well, Bobby O'Farrell's older brother got a job there last week so I went back and asked about my application."

Jan didn't wait for his mother to reply. "You know what they told me? They said that my application was misfiled and that they had filled all the available positions. Then I went over to Home Depot. The man said I wasn't strong enough to unload the trucks. I know he was lying 'cause they've got *girls* working there. The answer is the same everywhere. NO!"

Jan was sweating. He was red faced and on the edge of tears. He took a plastic cup from the cupboard and went to the faucet. He stared down at the sink, the once white porcelain worn away by years of scrubbing.

"I just don't believe you've tried hard enough," his mom said.

Jan flung the plastic cup into the sink with a force that surprised both of them. Whirling around, he leaned forward across the table and slammed both hands, palms down, on the metal.

Recklessly, he shouted. "I don't give a fuck what you believe! I'm eighteen. This is going to go down with or without you!"

Joy stood motionless. He couldn't tell if she was preparing to slug him or break down. He softened his tone. His voice was hoarse from shouting.

"Why not make it easier on yourself? All the money you've borrowed is gone, and all you have now is debt and worry."

Joy sagged into a vinyl-covered chair. She wanted to cry but the tears wouldn't come. She knew she should be thinking about her son and this pervert and what it implied, but her mind kept coming back to money.

Jan went around the table. He knelt and put his head in her lap. "Help me do this."

Joy was filled with self-reproach. "How can I agree to sell my own baby?" she murmured.

"Mom, I'm not a baby. And besides, it's not like I'm being carried off in a slave ship. Philadelphia isn't the backside of Mars. We can still see each other." Jan knew that was probably not in the cards but he didn't know what else to say.

The front door banged shut. "We're home!" shouted Daniel.

They both looked up at the faux Coca-Cola clock hanging over the stove. Had they really been at this for two hours?

Daniel and the girls came into the kitchen. Sara looked from her mother to Jan, then back to her mother again.

"What's going on? What's wrong?"

Joy put on her sad face.

"Jan is going to be moving out soon. We've been talking about it. We're very upset," she said.

"Jan, is it true?" Daniel asked. "Why do you have to go away?"

"The job I've got isn't around here, Danny," he answered.

The girls stood and looked at that their mother for some sign that everything was really was going to be alright. Ruth hurried around the table to Jan.

"Are you in trouble?" she asked.

"Is Jan gonna be okay?" Paula added, looking at their mother.

"Of course, he is, sweetheart. It's just upsetting, that's all."

Sara remained silent. She had seen the bus tickets Jan threw in the bathroom wastebasket. Round trip passes to Fifteenth and Van Wyck Streets. Unlike Jan, she had heard of the goings on up there and looked suspiciously at her brother.

"Jan, can I talk to you for a minute?" she asked him.

Grateful for the lull in the fighting, he followed his sister into the parlor.

Sara turned. "I think I know what's going on here."

Jan started to object then thought better of it.

"Oh, and what is that?"

"I found the bus ticket stubs in the wastebasket and I know what goes on up there on Van Wyck Street."

The back of Jan's calves began to quiver and he dropped into a chair.

"I won't say anything to the others, but you've gotta get out of here as soon as possible. You know what it's like here. If the neighbors find out about you they'll hang you from a basketball hoop and call it justice."

Before Jan could reply, Joy herded the kids into the hallway and called Sara to join them.

"It's getting late and this is a school night. You guys better get upstairs and get ready for bed," she ordered.

After the others had pounded up the worn stairs to the second-floor bedrooms, Joy took Jan back into the kitchen. "I'm not sure I'm going to go along with this. I'll have to think about it, but I'm not going to make up my mind until I meet this creep and even then I'll probably put my foot down. If the police get wind of this—"

Jan cut her off. "That won't happen."

"This is all wrong, Jan Christopher, and you know it!"

"What's wrong is you forced me into a situation I didn't ask for and now I'm being yelled at because I found an answer but you don't like it. But you're getting everything you want, all you have to do is take the money and run."

Joy looked as if she had been hit with a brick. Shock, rage and then guilt flashed across her face.

Jan reached out. "I'm sorry. Oh, God I'm so sorry. I didn't mean that!"

Joy shook him off without looking at him. "We're both tired. I've got to go to work tomorrow, and you've got to decide how you want to live the rest of your life. I'm going to bed. Good night."

He leaned over to kiss his mother on the cheek as he did every night. She pulled away in disgust.

Head bent low, Jan walked into the parlor and waited until he heard her close her bedroom door. He picked up the phone and dialed the number Tim had given him.

Tim answered on the second ring.

"It's me, I told her." Jan whispered. "She's hopping mad. She wants to meet you, but I think she's going to make trouble. What do I do now?"

Tim's voice was calm. He told Jan to bring his mother into the city after work. They would meet at the Adelphia Tavern in the Warwick Hotel on Locust Street. He said he would make a reservation in Jan's first name for seven o'clock sharp.

"I've never had a reservation made in my name before," Jan said quietly.

"See you at seven then; don't be late," Tim said.

"I'll be there," Jan answered.

The line went dead.

CHAPTER 9

▼

The following evening, Jan's mother came down the narrow stairs into the parlor. She was wearing the same dress she always wore to work, a simple cotton shift with white and yellow daises across the bodice.

"Why couldn't she wear something nicer?" Jan said to himself.

Even though he had graduated from Saint Dom's the previous month, he decided to wear his school uniform. They were his best clothes—a green blazer bearing Saint Dominic's seal, black twill pants, white shirt and green tie.

"Where the hell do you think you're going, the Cardinal's charity ball?" Joy snorted.

"I think this place might be kinda fancy," Jan said meekly

Her tone softened. "You've not had much, have you?"

Jan had no response. They both knew she had struggled to keep food and warmth for her family with little else in the way of the icing that other families had on their slice of life's cake. Still, Jan loved her and in spite of everything, believed she loved him too.

Jan was jerked from these thoughts when Joy barked,

"Okay, let's get going. SEPTA is the meanest bus line in the world. They don't wait for nobody!"

As they walked away from the house, Jan caught a movement from behind. Daniel was waving good-bye from the front door. He hadn't even noticed that his little brother had been in the room. How much he had gathered, Jan could only wonder. He jogged back and gave Daniel a hug; leaving him with a smile, he hurried after his mother.

The bus to Center City eased up to the curb and sagged to one side. The white paint was cancerous with rust and bore a coat of grit that defied even the power washing the night crews applied at the end of each day. It was a poor cousin to the gleaming coaches that sedately drove through the Society Hill section of Philadelphia.

Joy glared at the driver. "You know, pal, with the taxes I pay to this city you'd think they could at least clean the seats in here!"

"Lady, these seats are as clean as they'll ever be," replied the driver.

Tim's bedroom phone rang an hour before he was to leave for the Adelphia Tavern.

"This is Tim," he answered in his usual way.

The desk attendant's voice was all business. "Sir, there's a gentleman calling for you, a Mister Ward."

"Thank you, Jerry. Please ask him to have a seat in the lobby. I'll be right down."

A few minutes later Tim exited the elevator and walked to where Hansford Ward was eyeing a French watercolor completely hidden from anyone else's view by his massive frame. Han was a six foot seven, muscle man who hired himself out to any party who paid, government or private. Fighting wars for others had left him with a face only a mother could love. Scars ran up and down both cheeks. No one looking at him would suspect that he was an expert in the delicate art of Raku pottery, a craft he learned while working for a Japanese mobster. In Japan, he was considered a national treasure.

Hansford was known in the profession as Mr. Squeaks because of the squeaking noise his number twelve shoes made under the weight of his three hundred pound frame. Asked once if he was worried people would hear him coming and would lose the element of surprise, Han smiled and answered, "What do you think?" No one ever called him Mr. Squeaks to his face.

Tim forced a cough as he neared him. It was unwise to catch Han unawares.

Han had watched Tim's reflection in the glass covering the painting. He turned just as Tim reached him, extending his hand and offering what passed for a smile. They exchanged the usual greetings, then got down to business.

"So, Mr. M, who do you want me to hurt?" Han asked with a fake innocence.

"Don't get too disappointed, but it's nothing like that."

Tim knew he would not have to repeat his instructions once they were underway. And he knew Han could be relied on to say nothing about what he may or may not see or hear today.

Tim explained. "I've got a business deal with a woman at the Adelphia in about forty-five minutes. She will be with a young man and may try to cause a scene or even trouble. Your job is to make sure she doesn't even get a chance to make waves. Sit next to her while we discuss our business. That's all there is to it."

"Got it," Han said.

Tim handed him an envelope with one thousand dollars inside.

As the two men exited the Saint Roi, Han looked at Tim with a wry smile. "I know it's none of my business, Mr. M, but are you sure you want to get mixed up with a woman? You know when a man gets himself in deep trouble the French always say, *Recherché la femme!* Look for the woman!"

Tim smiled back at Han and said nothing.

The Adelphia Tavern, in the stately Warwick Hotel, was designed for private conversations between powerful men and women. Anyone needing to speak in confidence headed for its peaceful and secluded ambience. Each banquette was enclosed with walnut wainscoting reaching five feet from the floor. A pocket door, which could be closed or left open, added privacy if needed. All that was topped with two-foot frosted glass panels featuring turn of the century harness racing scenes. Subdued light reflecting off polished brass and waxed wood whispered, *Money.*

CHAPTER 10

▼

Jan and his mother walked in silence to the Warwick Hotel. A brass plaque beside the main door identified a narrow arch set in the dark marble as the entrance to the Adelphia Tavern. The happy hour rush was just beginning to wind down.

A man wearing an elegantly tailored suit approached Jan. After identifying himself to the maitre d' as having reservations, Jan and Joy were escorted to their booth. Jan wasn't sure if he should order anything, but the waiter assured him that his host had already provided a tab for anything they wished. Jan asked for a Coke. His mother declined.

Joy studied her son's face as he marveled at the splendid room. Her original intention was to put an end to this escapade, with the law if need be. Now she wasn't so sure. But before she could say anything, Tim and Han walked up and seated themselves without saying a word.

Jan looked from Tim to his mother and back again waiting for someone to speak.

Finally, Tim said, "Mrs. Phillips, my name is Tim and this is Mr. Ward. He is here as a witness to our contract."

Tim drew two envelopes from his inside jacket pocket. One contained a cashier's check for four thousand dollars. The other, a large envelope, held a single-page contract with places marked for her name and for a witness.

Joy shifted uncomfortably in what was left of her space at the table.

Tim held up his hand. "Please let me explain the terms you'll be agreeing to." Banking on Joy being ignorant of the legal niceties, he was confident she would believe anything he told her.

He pushed the bill of sale toward her. "For the sum of four grand you will sign the document before you, stating that you relinquish all claims and rights to the person named below and will further quit his life until such time as I deem it appropriate to alter the agreement. In short, you get four big ones to get permanently lost."

Jan sat rigid as a flagpole, his eyes pleading with Tim to be gentler. Joy looked away, then in a trembling voice asked, "How do I know you won't hurt my son?"

"If that was my game we wouldn't be sitting here," Tim said.

Joy looked at her son. "Jan, are you sure this is what you want?"

Tears watered his white shirt. Jan wanted to put his head on his mother's shoulder but thought better of it. He could smell the inexpensive perfume she bought off the sale counter at Eckerd's drugstore through his runny nose and tears.

"I love you Mom but I have to go. You said so yourself. Yes, I want to do this," he whispered.

Joy picked up the Mont Blanc pen Tim offered and signed the bottom line marked JP.

Tim handed the pen to Han, who had sat quietly observing the scene with fascination. He signed on the witness line and handed the pen and contract back to Tim.

"Where's my copy? I should get a copy!" she demanded.

"No copy for you. Once the check has cleared, it will indicate your full acceptance of the terms. As it happens tonight is Monday and the bank this is drawn on is open until ten p.m.. I suggest you get there as soon as possible. If you wish, Mr. Ward will go along to make sure you get there safely," Tim said.

Joy hung her head and meekly nodded her approval.

"One more thing," Tim added. "Mr. Ward may stop at your house to collect anything Jan may want from home. If that is the case, he will call you beforehand."

Joy started to object, but one stern look from Han stopped her.

Jan sat through as if he were watching a movie. Only the pitching of his stomach testified that it was really happening to him.

Tim looked around the table. "Well, as General McArthur once observed, These proceedings are concluded."

The two men stood and waited for Jan and his mother to follow.

Out on Locust Street Joy asked, "What now?"

"The bank is two blocks up and three over in the Penn Central Towers ground floor plaza," Tim answered. "A Mr. Tibbet is expecting you."

All four exchanged glances. Joy reached out and stroked Jan's cheek with the back of her hand. He reached up, took her hand and kissed it. A shudder racked his young frame, but he said nothing.

Tim put his arm around Jan as Han gently took Joy's elbow and guided her away.

"Will I ever see my family again?" Jan murmured.

"The native Americans say the paths of men cross many times," Tim said and led him back to the Saint Roi. It was getting late.

CHAPTER 11

▼

Joy Phillips walked to the bank office. Han accompanied her, his shoes making a squeaking sound like a baby bird's cry for food. She deposited her newly acquired wealth in an account that Tim had pre-arranged. How he'd managed to open an account in her name without her signature, she hadn't the faintest idea.

After they left the building, Han said, "I have my car in the lot here ma'am. May I carry you home?"

Joy studied Han's face. Her first impulse was to tell him to shove his car up his ass sideways. But fatigue won out over indignation. Her voice crushed with sadness, she said softly, "Yes, please. Thank you."

As they approached Han's Porsche convertible, Joy exclaimed, "My God, do you get in it or do you put it on?" She hadn't intended to make a joke, but Han doubled over in laughter. As they drove out of Center City Joy said, "Mr. Ward?"

"Please call me Han, ma'am. That would be short for Hansford. I'm off the clock as of now."

"Okay, Han," she replied. "May I ask you a question?"

"I'll answer it if I can ma'am."

"Will he be alright? He won't get into trouble or anything like that, will he?"

"Mr. M is a fine man," Han replied. "Your son will be fine as long as he does as he's told."

"Will I be able to see him sometimes?"

Han looked at Joy but made no reply.

"Then how about this? Will you…, I mean could you let me know how he's doing?" she pleaded. "I could give you my phone number."

"No, ma'am, I won't do that." Han sighed. "Look, if you go breaking your contract you'll have to give back the money, and there's no telling if you'll see your son even then."

Joy knew he was right. She still had a house full of kids to look after. She looked out the window. Her eyes were too clouded to see anything except blurs as the sports car shot down the narrow street. She gave way to a brief self-indulgent stab of guilt. She knew she was responsible for setting this in motion. Jan would never have done it on his own. On the plus side she had four thousand dollars in the bank and one less mouth to feed.

Han pulled up and parked outside Joy's house. The lights were on. That meant her kids would be home and ready for dinner.

"You take good care now," Han said. "As you know, I might be coming around to get some stuff for the young man."

Joy pulled herself out of the low seat. "Thank you, Han. If you do come around I just might have a pot of coffee on the stove."

"I'd like that, ma'am. Goodbye." With that, he drove off.

Dusk deepened into a long night for Joy Phillips.

CHAPTER 12

▼

As they entered the apartment, Jan heard a woman singing a Spanish lullaby.

"What's that?" he asked.

"That's Mrs. Santos. She's my housekeeper, and she cooks for me sometimes too."

"I call her Mrs. S, but I want you to call her Mrs. Santos. Also, she isn't a maid so you'll have to do your own laundry. And if you make a mess in the kitchen you'll be expected to wash up afterwards…got it?"

"Sure, I understand," Jan replied.

Yvonne Santos was widowed when her husband was murdered by one of General Pinochet's death squads in Chile. Fleeing with her only child, Sonya, she made her way to Philadelphia. With her Mundus Society, contacts Yvonne met Peter de Main.

Mrs. Santos emerged from the kitchen wearing a long apron with Japanese calligraphy stenciled across the top. Under the apron, she wore a beige dress of fine French cotton. She was a tall woman with straight black hair curled behind her ears. Widowed for decades, she still revered her murdered husband by wearing her wedding ring,

"Mrs. Santos," Tim said. "I want you to meet Jan. He'll be staying here."

She welcomed Jan with a warm smile.

"Do you speak Spanish?" she asked.

"I'm afraid I only know the bad words," Jan confessed.

"Not to worry, we can fix that! Eh, *Señor* Tim?"

"I'm sure we can. Is there any food for hungry lads tonight?' he asked.

"*Sí*. Everything is ready in the kitchen. I must go now before my bus is gone without me. I will see you *mañana*."

She slipped from the apartment without a sound while Tim led Jan into the kitchen.

Mrs. Santos had prepared a platter of roast duck surrounded by a chilled salad of haricot vert and a side dish of warm mashed potatoes.

"I hope you like breast of duck," Tim said.

"Oh, sure. We have it all the time in Kensington," Jan said sarcastically.

"I'm sorry. I didn't mean to put you down. It's just that I don't know how you've lived. I thought with a Catholic school education you would have had a chance to experience a bit of the world outside of Kensington."

"What I got was boxed ears and tough assignments."

"Boxed ears? I thought that went out with the new church."

"They got rid of the stuff that was harmless and kept the mean things. We all called our homeroom teacher, Sister Joe Fraser!"

"What about field trips?" Tim asked.

"The school got to go to some, but there was never enough money for me to go with my class."

Jan screwed up his courage. "What's going to happen to me Tim? Are you going to hurt me or something?"

"If you mean am I going to hit you or lock you up and make you a slave, the answer is no. However, I do want you to be submissive. If I want you to do something, I expect you to obey without any sass. Do you understand me?"

"Yes," Jan answered quietly.

Tim said, "Look, being a virgin, you will find some discomfort with what we do at first. Some of it you may never learn to enjoy, but as long as I'm having fun I expect you to grin and bear it."

Jan blushed. "Will I have to wear a dress with make-up and stuff?"

The question took Tim by surprise. "I like my sex to be with males," he answered gruffly. "If I wanted a girl I'd get one. Besides I like women too much to make parodies of them."

Jan nodded absently.

The meal was delicious, and Jan was surprised he even liked the beans. Normally he wouldn't eat them, but then he'd never had green beans like these.

They scraped the plates and Tim loaded the dishwasher.

"Follow me," he ordered.

CHAPTER 13

▼

Jan followed Tim down the wide hallway. They passed the bathroom where his wet clothes had dried the day before. Directly across the hall from this bathroom was a guestroom. Jan got only a glimpse in passing by, but he recognized the décor as Shaker because his mother had magazines featuring reproductions of their work. She had always admired its clean line even if she had no hope of ever affording it. On rainy days she would sit with him pouring over the dog eared magazines pointing out the styles she liked. In this way she had unwittingly instilled in her son a longing for things far beyond his means. Next was another bedroom, reserved for Mrs. Santos in case she needed to spend the night. It too offered the aesthetic of unadorned grace.

Tim stopped at the end of the hall and opened a doublewide door covered in tufted navy blue baize. The door's reverse side was covered in the same material. Tim ushered Jan into a room that was forty feet long and thirty-five feet wide.

"This is what they must mean by master bedroom," Jan thought.

The room was divided by a floor-to-ceiling movable partition that formed a dressing area complete with a wall of built-in armoires. Another area beyond was Tim's lounge. Jan wandered around the room looking at the props wealthy men use to make themselves comfortable. At last he came to the bed itself. It was a massive double king-size swathed with silk panels hanging from rings set in the ceiling. It almost looked like a tent pitched amidst a jungle of luxury.

Jan hadn't noticed Tim behind him and was startled when the silence broke. "Okay, strip!" Tim barked. He had dropped into a velvet-covered side chair and was smiling as he unbuttoned his shirt.

Jan hesitated ever so slightly before slipping off his school blazer. Again he was nervous and scared but now his stomach heaved with excitement. He looked around for a place to lay his clothes.

"Stop," Tim commanded.

A glimmer of relief crossed Jan's face.

"Fold all your clothes as you strip and stack them on the floor."

His expression crumpled, he continued.

Tim held his breath as Jan unbuttoned his shirt and showed a hairless chest with small, pink nipples. His skin was creamy white, not pasty like so many ill-fed boys of the inner city. Tim noticed for the first time how delicate his hands were. "The fingers of a pianist," he thought.

Jan knelt and folded each piece of clothing before standing to strip off his underpants. His hands shook as he slipped them down. He was totally smooth, having shaved the pale yellow hair from around his crotch earlier that day.

Tim was surprised to see he was partially circumcised. He hadn't noticed it before.

Jan crouched around his clothes wishing they would magically leap back to cover him. Once again in this house, he was naked and ashamed. Wondering if he would ever get used to this, he stared at Tim without expression as his heartbeat drummed in panic.

Tim studied Jan's young body. He looked pure and sweet, like an offering to the gods. If there was a flaw in the skin he couldn't see it.

Jan didn't know if he was supposed to say or do something.

Tim broke the silence, "I want you."

"What? I mean, excuse me?"

"I said, I want you to jack yourself off."

Jan tried to process the reality of Tim's words. Suddenly, what Jan had built up in his mind was in motion, and he didn't know where it would lead him or how he was supposed to act.

Tim had removed his shirt, revealing a firm but not hard chest. His dark summer tan had faded into a creamy brown.

Jan's eyes flickered for a moment. He didn't know if he could do this. It still seemed wrong—but something stirred deep inside him, like a tightening and at he same time a melting taste in his mouth. As apprehensive as he was, his body began to betray his growing desire. Jan's hand inched to the root of his arousal.

He began to gently caress himself. he stood quivering under Tim's lustful gaze.

His hand slid faster and faster until almost without warning he felt himself flare and burst with relief and pleasure.

Jan looked up at Tim embarrassed, unsure again, looking for approval. It was over. He got his show.

"Can I go now?" he asked sullenly.

"No," Tim growled.

Jan's lower lip trembled with frustrated rage. He glowered at Tim and started to get up.

"I need to clean up."

Tim moved to where Jan sat with his back propped against the bed's footboard.

"Wait! We're not finished. Open!" Tim ordered his voice husky with lust.

Jan drew back, shaking his head.

Tim snatched a handful of Jan's yellow hair and forced himself into Jan. He didn't stop until he had emptied himself.

Jan sat quietly sobbing.

Tim pointed Jan to the master bathroom. "Go and shower. There are towels on the warming rack. When you're finished just put the damp ones in the hamper."

Jan scampered away, quickly shutting the door behind him.

He slumped against the wall. He thought he was going to go mad. This place was wonderful, but at what price? Tim could be gentle but then suddenly harsh. Did he like him or not?

"Was this guy playing some sort of game? Is all this for real?" he wondered.

Too confused to think anymore he turned his attention to his surroundings. The master bath was something out of a Roman spa. Tim had it specially designed, including double-sized marble tubs with outlets for water massages. A shower stall was fitted with similar jets arranged up and down the walls. The marble and alabaster walls were decorated with scenes from the battle of Actium. Tim had them copied from ancient renderings found on Antony and Cleopatra's sarcophagi

As Jan entered the shower stall, it sprang to life with a soapy spray that began at his neck and swirled all the way down to his ankles. He turned and as if by magic a fine water spray rinsed away the gelée mix. It wasn't until then that Jan noticed six infrared lights set into the marble. Testing the light beams with his hand he learned he could control temperature, nozzle direction and gelée. He was overwhelmed.

"This guy can have anything and anybody. He won't want me for long," Jan said to the spray.

Sadness and despair pummeled his heart. Slumping to the shower floor, he began to cry. He hoped that the sound of water would drown out his sobs.

Tim slipped between the silk sheets, the gas log fireplace providing the room's only illumination. As he lay there, Tim could hear Jan weeping. He knew that sound well. More than fifteen years ago when he first came to the apartment he had wept bitterly too.

CHAPTER 14

▼

Jan finished his shower and dried himself with a bath sheet he found on the warming rack. He searched the bathroom for the hamper and founded it stowed behind a marble panel. Taking a deep breath, he opened the bathroom door, switched off the lights and walked into the bedroom, across the plush carpeting to the side of the bed. The softly glowing fireplace left just enough light in the room for navigation. Still, Tim could see Jan's naked form moving toward the bed. Jan was aware of his gaze. What they had done together a mere thirty minutes before didn't lessen his embarrassment.

As he approached the bed, Tim told him, "Come closer."

Reaching out with his left hand he fondled him. Jan stood shaking, partly with modesty and partly with new arousal. He still hadn't come to grips with the reality that, at least in his own mind, he was now just a fancy whore.

Finally, Tim released him and threw back the sheet. "Let's get some sleep," he said.

Jan was so relieved he didn't know whether to laugh or cry.

Tim fell back on to the oversize pillows, reached out and stroked Jan on the cheek.

"Try to sleep. We have a busy day tomorrow," he whispered.

Hoping it would please him, Jan curled into Tim's arms, certain sleep would elude him but physical and emotional exhaustion finally won over nerves. Jan awoke several times in the night, sat up and looked around the room. He needed to assure himself that this was not a dream. Pale moonlight filtered through the silk sheer curtains, throwing wild shadows across the bed. Jan wasn't afraid of the dark, but this was a little weird.

*   *   *   *

In the morning, Tim roused him with a kiss.

"The day is broke. Look about," he whispered into Jan's ear.

"Do you always quote Shakespeare in the morning?"

"Didn't you tell me you liked the Bard?"

"I love him." Jan yawned and stretched his arms.

"Do you think you could eat some breakfast? I'm starved," Tim said. He drew Jan into his arms, nuzzling him with his early-morning beard.

"Ugh…. Tim! What time is it?"

"Almost eight. Mrs. Santos will be arriving soon. What would you like for breakfast?"

"Anything is fine for me. I usually just stop at a corner store and get a Tasty Cake and some milk."

"I don't think we have any Tasty Cakes in the house. How about pancakes?"

"Pancakes are good. I don't get them very often."

Tim went into the bathroom to shave and shower. Jan took the opportunity to slip into his school pants and shirt before Tim came out. He left the bedroom and walked down the hall to the kitchen, where Mrs. Santos was setting china on the table.

"Good morning Mrs. Santos."

"*Buenos días, muchacho.* Did you sleep well last night?"

"It's a little difficult trying to sleep in a new bed," Jan answered.

Actually, Jan had never slept in any bed other than his own.

"What's this?" Jan asked, dipping a finger into a bowl filled with brown batter.

"*Ai, muchacho!*" she exclaimed. "No little ones in the kitchen until I'm ready to serve the food. That is for the pancakes."

"But Mrs. Santos, pancakes are supposed to be white, not brown."

"These are made with buckwheat flour. They are *Señor* Tim's favorite."

"Better stay out of the lady's path when she's cooking if you expect to eat," Tim said as he joined them.

Pointing with a wooden spoon to a chair closest to the wall, the housekeeper said, "Jan, you may sit here."

He sat and watched her prepare the pancakes.

"Do you prefer coffee, milk, tea or cocoa to drink?" she asked, offering Jan a plate stacked with silver dollar-sized cakes.

"Milk, please. I haven't gotten a taste for coffee yet."

"I have some delicious Costa Rican coffee, very mild. I'll bring some tomorrow and you can try it."

"Thank you, Mrs. Santos." Jan smiled. He liked her.

They two ate in silence. As Mrs. Santos began to clear away the plates Tim said, "Jan even though it's Tuesday, I think I can get you off school just for today. We can make arrangements for you to be taken to Saint Dominic's before the week is out. Until then I can drive you to school."

"I guess I didn't tell you that I graduated from school last month. Father Sobinski arranged for me to finish early by cramming my classes all into last summer. He wanted to make sure I got all my credits before he left the school. I really didn't think I was going to be able to make it since there was so little time to study and so much to learn. He must've known that he was going to be transferred to Rome, but he didn't tell me until the last minute. It really pissed me off."

Mrs. Santos turned slightly and looked at Tim, who arched an eyebrow and frowned at Jan. Pissed was not a word often heard in the house.

Jan apologized, "Sorry I didn't mean to be out of line."

"Don't worry too much about it. But I would like it if you would keep a lid on some of the language," Tim said.

Jan sat in embarrassed misery until Mrs. Santos reached over to give him a forgiving pat on the head.

"Okay. You two, *vaya. Vaya*! I have work to do!" she ordered.

Walking out of the kitchen Tim said, "Come with me and I'll show you the rest of the apartment."

There were only two rooms Jan hadn't seen, the office and a study. Both were the same twenty feet square in area. The office was furnished with vintage Danish modern pieces, which Tim had gotten at an estate sale. It boasted a partner's desk designed by Heywood Wakefield and a brace of yellow leather club chairs by Le Corbusier. Jan, of course, was completely ignorant of these fine details but would come to appreciate them in time.

Immediately drawn to the computer, he was amazed to see the monitor hanging on the wall rather than sitting on the desk.

"Wow! "That is so cool!" he said. "They have these hanging from the beams in stores for advertising and stuff, but I didn't know you can get them for home use. It must have cost a fortune!"

Tim smiled. "Come on, we have one more room to see." He guided Jan from the office to the study. Unlike the other rooms, this one had not been altered from its original art deco style. The walls were lined with bookshelves made of zebrawood. The floor was not like the uncovered parquet in the rest of the apartment but was made of dark green terrazzo, protected with a black and white wool rug in a zigzag motif. A signed print by Gustav Klimt hung over the fireplace.

Jan approached the picture and craned his neck, imitating the position of the subjects. "What are they doing?" he asked, stumped by the couple's pose.

"They're kissing."

"Kissing! Looks more like somebody's getting strangled to me!"

"It's called 'The Kiss', so that's what they're supposed to be doing," Tim explained.

"Well, I like the colors anyway," Jan said without enthusiasm.

Tim moved to the far end of the room. A large desk made of black acrylic occupied more that half the wall space. A 1932 Dominick Hall lamp of polished chrome stood alone on the bare surface.

Tim sat on the edge of the desk.

"Jan, if you've graduated from school, why did you wear your school clothes here? I'm sure you have other clothes, don't you?"

"My uniform is the best set I've got. I thought it would be okay. Did I do something wrong?"

"No, of course not."

"Tim, can I ask you a question?"

"Sure."

"Does Mrs. Santos know what's going on between us?"

"Jan, Mrs. S knows everything. Are you okay with that?"

"Yeah…, I guess so. It's just a little weird, you know. It's like, I don't know any adults who can deal with gay stuff."

"Jan, there are lots of straight people who wish us well."

"Not in Kensington there aren't!"

Tim pulled the chrome and black leather chair from the desk.

"There's a pen and pad in the side drawer. I want you to write down all your clothing sizes, shoes too. Oh, and your waist measurement. I'll be back in a minute."

Tim left Jan to make his list and returned to the kitchen to inform Mrs. Santos that he and Jan would be dining out that evening and that she didn't have to cook dinner for them.

Tim got back to the study just as Jan finished.

"Here," Jan said, handing over the list.

Tim scanned it, picked up the telephone and dialed.

A smooth voice answered. "Brooks Brothers department store, this is Anthony. How may I help you?"

"Anthony, this is Tim Morris at the Saint Roi. I'd like to place an order."

"Yes, sir, Mr. Morris what can I get for you?"

"I require five pairs of slacks; three pairs with pleats and two pair plain front. These are for a young fellow, so please don't send anything too dull looking."

"Certainly, not a problem. Will there be anything else?" Anthony asked.

"Yes, I need seven shirts, five button-down Oxford cloths, in pink, yellow, white and blue. The other two shirts I want in silk, one sage green the other in a wine color if you happen to have them in stock. Also, I need fourteen pair of jockey shorts and socks. Also, send over three belts, one black, one tan and one gray. For shoes I'll need one pair of cordovan loafers and one pair of black lace ups with a plain-capped toe."

Tim repeated the sizes that Jan had written.

"Oh, and Anthony, do you know if Mr. de Silva is available to do alterations this afternoon? I would really like to get these items ready to wear as soon as possible."

Anthony replied quickly, "I happen to know that Mr. de Silva has a free schedule this afternoon. Would three o'clock be convenient for you? Also, I can send over a wide selection of pants and you can select the colors yourself. I assume you'll want the pleated styles to be fully lined as usual."

"Yes, that would be perfect. Thank you, Anthony," Tim said.

Switching off the telephone handset, Tim turned to Jan. "Well, we're all set, but we still need to get you some jeans and sneakers. You can't look like you're going to a school dance every day."

Jan looked down into his lap. He didn't know what to say.

He got up from the swivel chair. He stepped over to Tim, put his arms around the man's waist, and rested his head on Tim's shoulder. The gesture was the only way that he knew to say thank you, at least the only way he felt he could say it without trying to search for words that would sound stupid or even worse, insincere.

"C'mon, let's get going. The day is going to get away from us," Tim said.

They said goodbye to Mrs. Santos and walked to the elevator for the short ride to the lobby. Out on the street the workday was in full swing as small knots of people pushed their way up the sidewalks. Drivers honked impatience at pedestrians. Life was everywhere.

"I don't have to go to school anymore, but don't you have a job you have to go to?" Jan asked.

"Well," replied Tim. "I do have a job to go to, but since I own the company I get to go in whenever I want, and half the time I'm really not needed there. The place runs very smoothly without me. I hate to admit it, but it's true. It's a good thing I'm the one who signs the paychecks or else they'd probably try to get rid of me," he laughed.

"You know where the Gap is on Walnut Street, right?" Tim asked.

"Sure I do. The bus out to Kensington goes down Walnut Street before heading out of town."

They cut through the park at Rittenhouse Square and crossed Walnut Street to the Gap clothing store. A store attendant held the door as Jan and Tim passed into the world of teen couture. Jan had been in the Gap at Penn's Landing, but this store was much fancier.

"Go pick out some jeans; five pair should be enough. After that we'll go over to the J. Crew store and look for some sweaters and sneakers," Tim said.

Jan was so excited he felt like skipping down the aisle. Instead, he let his heart do the skipping for him. Thirty minutes of careful thought ended in his settling on faded stonewashed button-fly 501s—snug fit of course.

Tim handed Jan one hundred sixty dollars to pay for the jeans. When Jan looked puzzled, Tim told him, "I don't want you to feel embarrassed by having me hand over the cash."

Jan nodded. Tim also didn't want to remind Jan that there were such things as debit cards. He felt he could trust him, but there were limits to their arrangement and this was one of them.

From there, they walked over to Market Street and into the J. Crew store. Tim helped Jan pick out four rolled-neck wool sweaters and a V-neck with cable stitching down the front.

It was getting close lunchtime. Tim's stomach was beginning to growl. Foot traffic on Market Street had picked up as office workers made a dash for lunch.

"I'm hungry," he said. "How about you?"

"Yeah, I am too." Jan was so overwhelmed with shopping that he had hardly thought about food

"There's a really cool restaurant on Walnut Street just down from Rittenhouse Square. A friend of my mom's took us there for her birthday one time. They even have a wall that's actually a waterfall!"

"I know where you mean! It's called The Good Earth. They specialize in Asian and French cuisine. Would you like to go there?"

"Could we really?"

"We won't be eating dinner until eight o'clock or so tonight anyway, so we'd better get a hearty meal now." As they walked toward Walnut Street, they pushed past a group of secretaries lined up to buy soft pretzels. Braids of hot bread, thick with coarse salt, hung from wooden dowels in carts at every intersection.

"Ugh!" Jan muttered under his breath. "I don't know what people see in those things. Whenever my mom bought them for us all that soft dough would get stuck in my teeth. I hated it. Mom always thought it was a big treat to buy them for us, so of course I had to eat one. I didn't want to make her feel bad about it.

The memory of his mother made Jan feel a little melancholy. Tim sensed it and wrapped his arm around Jan's shoulders. He felt sadly reminiscent too but had learned long ago to chase unbidden memories out of his mind as quickly as they entered. They walked off at a brisk pace; carried along by the rush of the mid-day lunch crowd.

The sound of water gently falling was the first thing they heard when they passed through the glass stores of The Good Earth restaurant. The wall of shimmering water, thinly spread across green jade colored tiles, provided instant relief from the city's noontime hubbub.

A tall, elegant Chinese woman greeted them at the door. Her nametag read "Sophie." Yes, she informed them, they were in luck. There was a table available. Sophie led Tim and Jan to the rear of the dining room, where a small table for two stood with others of similar size, now crowded with feasting couples.

Ochre-colored terracotta walls soared three stories above the floor hemming in the space. Into one side of the far wall, a carved niche housed a giant golden Buddha. Ferns, iridescent with spay from the fountain, were set high in the wall and softened what would have been an otherwise stark room.

Jan's excitement was almost palpable. Tim was excited too; the more time he spent with Jan the more he thought that Jan might turn out to be his salvation. Their waiter arrived, announced that his name was Akira and that he would be their server.

Tim smiled and said, "Well, Akira, my name is Tim and this is Jan and we will be your customers."

Akira was confused at first, and then gave a broad smile. "That is a good joke," he said.

Tim decided on Mongolian lamb with plain white rice and green tea. Jan tried valiantly to pronounce the Korean word for his selection, fumbling through several renditions before he ended up with something that sounded like bee-bop.

Akira, accustomed to westerners not being able to pronounce some Asian words, said nothing to embarrass his customer.

"How did I do?" he asked after Akira had left with their orders.

"Sounded okay to me!" Tim said.

Jan and Tim worked through their lunches keeping the conversation mostly on the light side. They discovered that they both liked action movies like *K19* and *The Matrix*.

They talked about English mystery dramas on TV but with less enthusiasm on Jan's part. Tim asked Jan if he liked watching the History Channel. Jan confessed that he didn't.

"History is something you really should try to learn about. History is the story of ourselves. If you don't know where you've been, you can't possibly know where you're going. It's not just learning about dates and wars but seeing the whole thread of civilization as a continuous event."

"Well, yeah, but what has that got to do with me now?" Jan asked.

"Knowing and understanding why the men and women of the past behaved they way they did and why they made the decisions they did helps us make sense of the world of today. All of us, live with the results of decisions made over centuries by important people...and some not so important ones too

Jan listened as Tim continued. "Now with separate and diverse cultures becoming more interconnected, it's important that all of us know our neighbor, and know him well. You see, the hardest part of all this is for people to make the leap from living as single nations to living as global communities with common interests. That doesn't mean giving up identities but giving up the fear of losing those identities. There are nations and groups who, for whatever reason, continue to live in the ninth century but with twenty first century technologies at hand. In some cases, it's proved to be a deadly combination."

Jan thought about this for a while. "You know, I wish I had had a teacher like you to explain why studying is important. I was really bored with school. Looking back, I guess I really didn't know why I was there."

"Jan, ninety percent of living well is learning each day how to be a good neighbor. You never stop learning, not just big stuff either. Little things make up life too. You'll see what I mean in time."

Tim looked at his watch. "It's getting close to 2 o'clock. We'd better get back home. We don't want to keep Mr. de Silva waiting."

He paid the bill, including a generous tip for Akira. "Who says lawyers are poor tippers?" he said, winking at Jan.

CHAPTER 15

▼

Jan burst into the apartment with Tim close behind.

"Mrs. Santos!" Jan called out excitedly. "We went to the most awesome Asian restaurant for lunch. Tim tried to teach me how to use chopsticks…but I'm no good at it."

Mrs. Santos chuckled as she dried her hands on a dishtowel." We have some here so you can practice for the next time," she said.

"*Señor* Tim, Mr. de Silva called. He will be here in about ten minutes."

"Thanks Mrs. S, could you please put Jan's new things in the empty armoire in the master bedroom."

Jan followed Mrs. Santos while Tim went to the office, shut the door and flipped a switch to a small yellow light located next to the knob on the outside door jam. The office and master bedroom had the same feature. When that light was on, he was not to be disturbed–by anyone. Tim locked the door, walked to the Wakefield desk and retrieved the agreement Joy Phillips had signed the day before. He walked over to the fire place, stuffing the paper between the logs. Tim wondered if he did the right thing by cutting Joy out of Jan's life. A woman in Joy's position could potentially be a mill stone around their necks. Tim had plans for Jan and a meddling mother might derail them. No, he decided, his original plan was best for all concerned.

Roberto de Silva was a short, stocky man with a neat pencil moustache and slicked-back hair. He had been tailoring Brooks Brothers clients for forty years. Those who didn't know him well thought he seemed stiff and unapproachable.

In fact, he was dedicated, serious-minded and the very best tailor a fellow could hope for.

Once, an unsuspecting junior sales clerk asked him if he ever thought of retiring.

"And just who do you think would dress the men in this town if I did such a foolish thing?" he snapped.

De Silva breezed through the door like an impresario about to conduct Mozart. He had two assistants in tow, each pushing wheeled clothing racks. They stood sentry silent as their boss and Tim exchanged greetings.

"*Señor* Morris, what an honor it is to serve you again!" "Thank you, Mr. de Silva. As you can see we have a lot to do today," Tim said.

"Do not worry, señor. We will be, as they say, swift as the hare."

"That is quick as a bunny, Roberto," Mrs. Santos said in joining the men.

Roberto de Silva gave a deep bow. "*Señora,* you are more lovely than the last time I saw you!"

"The last time we met was yesterday at Mass, Roberto."

"Ah, *señora,* but as the song says, what a difference a day makes!"

Mrs. Santos laughed and returned to the kitchen shaking her head.

Jan took all this repartee in like a dry sponge. The conversation between de Silva and Tim was courteous yet formal. The interaction between the two Latinos was that of old friends. Jan was learning.

"Mr. de Silva, I want you to meet Jan. He's the one you'll be measuring for today."

Jan started to offer his hand to shake but a look from Tim told him this was unnecessary.

"Pleased to meet you, sir," Jan said.

Tim smiled approvingly.

"*Mucho gusto,*" replied de Silva.

Turning to Tim, the tailor said, "*Señor* Morris, I have taken the great liberty of bringing also a selection of suits that might interest you."

"Mr. de Silva, you are a lifesaver! I had completely forgotten about a suit. As a matter of fact I'll need a tuxedo too."

"Tuxedo!" Jan thought.

De Silva turned to Jan, "Then let us begin, *señor.*"

As de Silva busied himself with laying out pants so that Jan could select the fabrics he liked best, his assistants spread the shirts, socks and underwear out on the sofa.

Mrs. Santos decided to call it a day.

"*Señor* Tim, if there is nothing else you require, I will be going now."

"Nothing for now. Thank you, Mrs. S. See you tomorrow," he answered.

Tim looked on as Jan selected flannel pants in black and charcoal gray. Then the assistants offered Jan light colors of buff and khaki in a cloth he had never felt before.

"What is this made of?" he whispered to the younger of the two.

"It's called moleskin."

"Cool."

Jan tugged at the satin lining in the pants. "There's something wrong here, Tim."

Tim looked and suddenly realized Jan had never seen lined pants before.

"That's the lining," he replied softly.

"Lined? You mean, like my school blazer?" he asked.

Tim nodded a yes.

"Holy smokes," Jan said, awed by the elegance of the garments. Jan was liking the way rich people live!

De Silva pulled out two shoeboxes. He chose the black lace-up style and asked Jan to try them on for fit.

Walking around the room, Jan finally pronounced them comfortable as slippers. The same verdict was delivered on the cordovan loafers.

"Good. Then we'll use the loafers, since they are easier to change in and out of while I measure for the cuffs and hems."

As the assistants handed the pants to Jan, he changed from one pair to another. The master tailor measured and pinned with a speed envied by hopeful students of the craft.

"All finished," he announced, then added, "*Señor* Morris, I will personally return with the altered pieces to ensure they are correct in every way."

"Thank you, gentlemen," Tim said to the trio as he ushered them out.

Jan stood by the sofa gathering up the underwear and socks. Tim came to him, took the armload of clothing, tossed the bundle back on the cushions and pulled Jan into his arms.

Jan's mouth yielded to Tim's strong kiss. They stood holding each other before Tim said, "Come on, we need a shower before dinner."

CHAPTER 16

▼

Tim led Jan by the hand down the hall into the master bedroom. The late afternoon sunlight filtered through the sheer curtains, turning the walls into shimmering shadows of gold. Jan stood very still as Tim caressed his hair and neck. He began unbuttoning Jan's shirt.

Jan nervously reached out and followed Tim's lead. Small beads of perspiration dotted his upper lip.

Tim put his hand behind Jan's neck and drew his lips into another deep kiss. Returning Tim's kiss he hoping he was doing it well. Aside from his mother, Jan had never kissed anyone before he met Tim—and he had never kissed anyone like this.

Releasing him, Tim slipped Jan's shirt off and let it fall.

Jan imitated Tim and, without coaxing, leaned into his chest kissing one of Tim's nipples. Then slowly, ever so slowly he opened his mouth and took the hard knot of flesh between his lips. He had no way of knowing if Tim would like this. A moan of pleasure told Jan that he did.

Tim's hand gently slipped to Jan's crotch. He massaged Jan's growing arousal beneath the fabric, then moved his hands up and opened Jan's pants. Tim's light touch made Jan sigh and reveal his need but Tim wasn't ready for this to be over too soon.

"Ah, the impatience of youth," Tim mused.

Tim moved his hands around to Jan's back. He gradually worked his hands down to his waist, pulling Jan's jockey shorts down. The briefs slipped to the floor. Jan swayed and felt as if he were going to faint.

Tim abruptly placed his hands on the boy's shoulders and pushed down.

Jan's knees bent. He sagged to the floor. He reached out, touching the fabric with just his fingertips. He breathed Tim's scent and could feel the heat of Tim's hard body. Jan wondered if his body felt as hot to Tim.

Tim put his hand behind Jan's head and slowly pushed the boy's face into his crotch. Jan mouthed Tim's lust through the cloth. Reaching up Jan drew the shorts off Tim's hips.

"Let me—" he said, moving his mouth closer, but Tim took Jan by the arms and brought him to his feet.

"Let's get a shower; it's getting close to dinner time. There's someone I want you to meet."

Jan nearly screamed with frustration. "I don't understand you! First you want it, and then you don't! Just when I start to get comfortable you pull away!"

"Oh, I think you'll appreciate the anticipation well enough tonight." Tim assured him.

Begrudgingly Jan made for the bathroom and the shower with Tim behind him.

The shower could easily hold four people. The water nozzles, directed so that a curtain or door was unnecessary, sprang to life as they entered the stall. Warm soapy water enveloped them, and they swayed in each other's arms.

Jan hugged Tim stiffly.

"Are you okay?" Tim asked.

"Yeah. It's just I feel...well...kinda 'emotional' but I'm not sure what to call it...yet. You confuse me."

He held Tim closer.

Tim didn't realize that Jan had mastered the water controls and got a jolt of cold water up his backside when Jan, with a slight hand motion, turned Tim's side of the shower into a cold rinse.

"Arrggg!" Tim laughed.

"Serves you right for teasing me like that!" Jan shot back.

Jan raced into the bedroom, snatching a bath sheet from the rack.

Tim followed, drying his hair. He grabbed a pair of jeans from the armoire and said, "The place we're headed to for dinner is casual, so jeans are okay."

Jan's new 501s caught at his slender hips and were just long enough to make a puddle of denim around his ankles. A loose-fitting, dark green wool sweater with a wide open, rolled collar showed off his pale skin. Plain white sneakers finished off the poor little rich kid look.

They headed to the Venture Inn, a bar and restaurant favored by gays for decades. Tim liked the Venture, not because of the menu or the prices, but because his longtime friend and partner in gossip was the bar manager.

Pat Hunter had been associated with the Venture for as long as Tim could remember. Rumor had it that he had been involved with the national political scene of the 1960s. He always demurred when pressed on this topic, yet he appeared to know everyone connected to the nation's capital. Tim knew the real story behind the rumors, and they were all true.

The Venture's main room was a simple rectangle divided roughly in equal parts, the dining room sectioned off from the bar area with a short wall. In the 1980s and '90s, designs ranged from the exposed beam industrial loft look to that of an English gentleman's club complete with faux oil paintings, swarming with horses and dogs. The latest redo was a watered-down version of art deco.

Pat commanded the bar's twenty-seven feet of mahogany, marble and brass like a pirate captain standing on a ship's deck, awash in seawater. He had never been to sea and frequently declared his belief that the only proper use for water was bathing. Nonetheless, it was an image he could appreciate. Pat had just learned from one of the regulars that the older gentleman at the end of the bar was a well-known TV evangelist. The preacher was trying very hard to seduce a twenty-something twink, a guy everyone knew was very available. After looking back and seeing the two of them gone, Pat had to assume they had left together. Ah, romance in the big city!

With Tim holding the heavy brown door, Jan nervously entered his very first bar, gay or straight. His class had read *Romeo and Juliet* during the last school semester. The phrase "palace of dim light" immediately came to his mind.

Voice levels in bars tend to be on par with those at baseball games, but as Jan took a few steps into the Inn, everyone stopped speaking. A deep quiet swept the room, as men broke off conversation in mid-sentence. Silence is eerie in a crowded bar. It's especially so when a dozen or so men drool over you like fat ladies at a buffet and you are the last slice of cake on the table.

Jan wanted to turn and run, but Tim simply put an arm round his shoulders and moved him toward the dining room.

Pat came from behind the business end of the bar waving a happy hello.

"Tim! Well, how are you doing? Where have you been? I've missed you!" he bellowed as he pumped Tim's hand.

Pat may have been addressing Tim, but he was eyeing Jan with a look that could strip the bark off a redwood.

"Pat," Tim said. "I want you to meet a special friend of mine. This is Jan."

"Your special friend? Oh, I see. Welcome to the Venture."

"It's good to be here," Jan replied, hoping to sound at ease.

Putting his eyes back into their sockets Pat grabbed two menus and said in his best butler's voice, "Follow me."

Pat's duties did not include acting as host for the dining room, but he had wanted to catch up on new gossip with Tim. But with Tim's new friend in tow, he knew that was not going to happen tonight.

Once they were settled down at their table, Jan excused himself to the restroom.

Tim indicated an unmarked door, and after he left caught Pat's sleeve.

"Listen, Pat. I want to ask a favor."

A concerned look crossed Pat's face. "Sure, Tim, anything at all. Is everything okay?"

"Yeah, everything's fine. I just want to be sure that if Jan needs you for any-thing, anything at all, I can count on you to come through, with no strings attached."

Pat knew what no strings meant. "No problem," he said, knowing exactly what Tim meant.

Jan returned just as the men concluded their agreement. He was a little red-faced and told them a man had followed him into the restroom and made a pass.

"There aren't any stalls or partitions in there! He could see me!" Jan com-plained.

"Uh, Jan, that's so people can…uh…how can I say this delicately. Get acquainted?" Pat answered.

"Oh, I see. I think from now on I'll just hold it when I'm here."

"That won't be necessary. I'll pass the word along that you're off-limits. No one will bother you again."

"Thanks."

Tim just chortled into his menu.

The food was good but not memorable. Tim ordered crab imperial and a glass of Chardonnay. Jan had never eaten shrimp scampi and afterwards voted it tasty but too salty.

Tim's purpose in bringing Jan to the Venture Inn was to introduce him to Pat. Mission accomplished, the two said their goodbyes and headed back to the Saint Roi. It was getting late.

CHAPTER 17

▼

They walked slowly along Van Wyck Street. Steam, smelling of earth and water, coiled from manhole covers. The vapors reached up as if to pull the dark sky down to Earth. The swirling haze made Jan think of cigarettes.

"Tim, I never asked, but you don't smoke anything, do you?"

"If you're asking about pot and other recreational drugs, the answer is no. How about you?"

"No way!" Jan said. "Father Sobinski would skin me alive and Sister Mary Rose would make baby toys from my bones if I ever tried that stuff."

Tim laughed.

"Go ahead and laugh, but there was this guy, Alexander Yhaski. He stole a pack of cigarettes from a corner drugstore. Mother Eileen caught us guys in the locker room just when he was about to show us how to smoke. When we all got back into class, she made him stand up in front of the whole class and eat the cigarettes, even the filters. He got real sick and threw-up all over the floor. Then she made him get a mop and bucket from the janitor's closet and clean it up. He kept asking to see the school nurse, but she wouldn't let him until he finished. He was so sick that he even pissed himself. He never came back to Saint Dom's and I heard that he even tried to kill himself with pills. His best friend told me his mom and dad sent him to public school."

They stopped at the raised median that divides Broad Street, waiting as a massive street sweeper devoured the curb debris.

"So," Jan said, "to make a long story short, I was too scared to get into any of that stuff."

When Tim didn't respond Jan asked meekly, "So, um, Tim, have you ever tried it, I mean just so see what it was like?"

"I did when I was about fifteen. That's before I…well…it was before…." Tim broke off the topic. It was obvious that he didn't want to talk about his past.

Jan twisted his face into a question mark but let the subject drop.

The Saint Roi's lobby was empty at this time of night. Their footfalls sounded like cannon fire on the marble floor. The night desk clerk was studying a textbook and didn't look up as Jan and Tim passed.

The silence in the elevator begged to be broken. Jan took Tim's hand. "Thanks for the night out. I guess this is our first date."

"You could call it that. I wish we had met under different circumstances," Tim replied.

"If the circumstances were different we wouldn't have met at all," Jan answered.

The doors whooshed open, and they walked the few steps to the apartment door.

Jan was getting nervous as bedtime approached again.

"Jan, get out of those clothes and take a shower. I'll be in later. I have some work to do."

Jan moved off to the bedroom yawning.

Tim entered his study, turned on the no entry light, went to a row of leather bound books and selected the last one in line. All the books on this shelf were journals. The spine of each volume was chronologically dated, beginning in 1906. It had taken him nine years to read them and began his own in 1987, three months after he turned twenty-five.

Tim picked up a pen, dipped the gold tip into a brass inkwell and began to write. He hadn't made an entry since the second Sunday in September, the first day he saw Jan hanging round Van Wyck Street. Time flew by as Tim wrote out his thoughts. The mantle clock chimed two a.m. as he finished.

He closed the book and returned it to the shelf.

Switching off the lights, he tiptoed down the hall to the bedroom. Jan was lying face down, his naked body splayed across the bed, smooth legs intertwined in the black silk sheets. Tim stood for a while just looking at him. Jan's silvery flesh looked like pearl enamel in the pale light. He went to the bathroom, stripped and bathed the odor of booze and smoke from his skin. After toweling himself dry he padded across the room and crawled onto the bed.

Jan stirred, scooted over and planted a misguided kiss in his ear, murmuring dreamily. "I waited for you as long as I could. Sorry."

"It's okay."

Tim turned to speak more, but the boy had already wandered back into the land of Nod. He watched as Jan's eyes flitted beneath paper-thin eyelids, then leaned back into the soft pillows and for the first time in years thought back to the day when he came to sleep in this room for the first time and the circumstances leading to his being in Philadelphia in the first place.

Tim was a tall, scrawny, smart-alecky kid. He was also very angry. He had changed from a zealous Pentecostal follower at fourteen to a cynical streetwise sixteen year old hustler. He hated everyone who used him and everyone who tried to be kind to him with equal ferocity. No one knew he was frightened too, scared stiff he was going to die in a ditch with a belly full of semen and a twenty dollar bill in his pocket. Not exactly the dream he had when he left Little Fork, West Virginia, and headed for New York City. His money, less than seventy-five dollars, got him as far as Philadelphia. It wasn't the Big Apple, but it was a large city full of opportunity.

It dawned on Tim that he was gay when he was fourteen and his mind turned to boys, not girls. His limited sexual fantasies were directed toward his best friend and a few guys at school. In his ignorance, he didn't realize there was anything out of the ordinary about it. Sex was never discussed, and so he had no idea that what he was feeling was considered wrong or ugly or even sinful by the people in his community.

Oddly enough, it was in church, rather than in a bed or behind the town drug store, that Tim first learned what homosexuality was.

The Tabernacle of the Unknown Tongues was one of those Pentecostal splinter congregations that accepted every word in the Good Book as if it were absolute truth, even when those words were in obvious conflict. The needy, frightened, devout, earnest souls who filled the pews lived in total spiritual isolation. Insulated from other Christian denominations by a harsh geography and a fierce suspicion of newfangled ideas, this Pentecostal gathering was certain that outsiders were at best sinners and at worst devils. Either way they were to be shunned as corrupting influences in God's community.

As a young boy, Tim was as devoted a follower of the church as you could get this side of heaven. His young mind was shaped by prayer meetings held in the tiny church, at home and at the Bible school he attended in lieu of public school.

The tent rallies conducted by visiting ministers claiming to heal the sick, all in the name of Jesus, would knock Tim to his knees.

"Oh the rapture, oh the rapture," he would cry out in frenzied ecstasy. He loved being in church; singing the hymns along with his younger brother and parents made him feel close to God.

Pastor Leo Robbins was a self-righteous bigot who got his ordination papers from a correspondence seminary operating out of a concrete block building in Wagoola Florida. In many of his sermons, Robbins had declared himself the Angel of the Bottomless Pit. Moreover, he told them that the Lord had commanded him to root out sin in his flock. Many in the congregation were left trembling after his diatribes. They said it was the Holy Ghost making them shake, but fear was a more likely cause.

One Sunday, Robbins was howling from his pulpit about the sin of Sodom. Tim knew about Sodom and Gomorrah but didn't have a clue as to what this terrible sin was.

After the service, Tim found the pastor in the church hall. He was sitting alone at a piano, picking out the chords of a hymn. Like many clergy, Robbins had learned music so he could lead and instruct his flock in songs of faith.

"Pastor," Tim said as he approached, "may I ask you something?"

"Tim Morris, you can ask me anything, and I'll answer it as best I can."

"I was wondering exactly what this great sin was that caused God to kill all those people in Sodom and Gomorrah. It doesn't say in the Bible exactly. I've studied the Word of the Lord a lot. I especially like the Letters of the Apostles," he added as if to show that he wasn't totally ignorant of the Scriptures.

The reverend looked at Tim, trying to figure out if this was true lack of understanding or an attempt to draw him into a lurid description of sex. It might be too that this boy wanted to talk about sex of any kind and had no one to ask about it.

Robbins decided to answer the question directly and see where it would lead.

"Well, the sin is homosexuality." Robbins waited for a reaction.

Tim looked as if he had never heard the word. In fact, until that moment, he hadn't. "I don't know what that is," he said honestly.

"Boy, you know about sex, don't you? I mean how babies are made?"

"Yes," Tim answered. "My mom told me about how she and dad made my little brother Mathew."

Robbins sighed in relief. At least he wouldn't have to cover that ground!

"Homosexuality is when two males or two females are attracted to one another and act out that attraction in a sexual way. This is a grave sin Boy. The Holy

Word tells us what the Lord of hosts did to the wicked Sodomites. He smote them in their evil city. He caused their flesh to melt and He threw them into the lake of fire from which there is no escape. That's what happens to homosexuals. It's right there in the Bible for everyone to read. The Lord's vengeance is swift and terrible to behold. The heavenly angels, the mightiest of His creation tremble in fear of The Wrath of the Lamb." The minister's voice tailed off in a reverie; in love with his own voice.

"You mean that if a guy sees another guy and…well you know…kinda likes it, then it's the sin of ho-mo-sex-u-ality?"

Pastor Robbins blinked. Tim's voice drew him back into the present.

"Ah, why yes, does that answer your question?"

Tim's eyes grew wide with fear in realizing he had always felt those desires.

"Pastor! Please don't say that God will strike me dead! I don't want my skin to melt off!" Tim cried.

Robbins grabbed Tim by the shoulders and shook him hard.

"Boy, what are you saying? Are you trying to confess to homosexuality?"

Tim was half out of his mind with grief and shame. He could only sob his answer.

"I don't know! It *is* what I think about."

"Boy," Robbins said with his voice trembling and his gaze locked on Tim's face, "this is a serious matter. I'll have to take it up with your parents and the church elders immediately!"

"Yes, sir," Tim whimpered. It was the only reply an obedient servant of God could make.

Without another word, Robbins swung around to the piano and banged out part of a hymn. *"When Thy judgment spreads destruction, keep us safe on Zion's hill."*

Tim staggered back, tripping over a folding chair. The clattering noise was drowned out by the piano's stormy hymn. He fled the church hall and ran home in time to wash up for the traditional Sunday supper of fried chicken, mashed potatoes, string beans, biscuits and gravy. It would be Tim's last Sunday supper with his parents.

He waited for the phone to ring. Eventually, he began to believe that Pastor Robbins had just meant to scare him. The call came just after eight o'clock.

His father answered the phone. When he replaced the receiver, he turned in a fury.

"What's wrong?" Tim's mother asked. "What's going on?"

Snatching the razor strap from behind the bathroom door, Mr. Morris, yelled, "That was Pastor Robbins. It seems we have a sodomite in our midst!

Pointing at Tim he shouted, "This son you bore me is queer! The reverend said he had no choice but to inform the church elders. By now it's all over town!"

His mother stood by wide eyed and watched as Tim was lashed with the razor strap. She clutched Tim's thirteen year-old brother to her as if to protect him from the Devil's contamination.

Great, wide welts rose up under the teen's flannel shirt, making it stick to his raw skin.

Tim ran from corner to corner in the small kitchen, crying and begging for the beating to stop. It didn't. The whipping continued until his father's arm tired.

"O God! Strengthen my arm as Ye did that of Joshua!" he cried.

"Daddy…please!" Tim sobbed. "I'm sorry…I'll be a good boy…daddy please don't hurt me…please stop!"

"I'll not have a sodomite in my house!" he screamed as he beat Satan out of the boy's soul, exorcising his own shame at having sired what he believed to be a hateful thing before the eyes of God. At the tender age of fourteen years and four months, Tim had become a hateful thing to his own father.

Tim was pushed into the room he shared with his brother. Over the next six days he was kept from school; not because his parents believed the kids would harm him but because they were ashamed and didn't know exactly what the elders would decide. They did have a pretty good idea, though. The whole family would be shunned, cut off from their church and its congregation or if they were lucky, only their son would be cast out.

His destruction was complete the following Sunday when he stood before the assembly of the saved and was denounced as unworthy of God's grace.

Pastor Robbins condemned Tim from the sanctuary.

"Timothy Morris alone has cast himself into the outer darkness where there is the weeping and gnashing of teeth," he shouted to the quaking throng.

Tim's family sat in silence as he was pronounced a non-member of the assembly. No one testified on his behalf. His punishment was set forth in Holy Scripture. Robbins handed a marked passage for Tim to read aloud.

He scanned the words that were supposed to justify their actions. "If your right hand offends thee, cut it off. If thy eye offends thee, pluck it out."

Tim put the Bible on the lectern and looked out at his self-righteous accusers. He decided to quote a different passage from memory. "What communion hath light with darkness? Wherefore come out from among them and be separate."

With those words, Timothy Harold Morris walked down the aisle and away from his beloved church.

The congregation was stunned at the audacity of such an act. They whispered among themselves, "Imagine a child, a child mind you, choosing his own text to read from the Book!"

While the followers congratulated Pastor Robbins on a moving service, Tim wandered home alone, truly alone. All his tears had been cried out the previous week. Earlier, he had stashed an Army surplus duffle bag in the garage with all his childhood possessions. Carrying everything he owned on his back, he moved off toward the highway.

Tim's parents returned home to find their fourteen year old son gone. No note was found. No police report for a missing child was made.

Tim rolled over and squeezed Jan in a warm hug. The clock's illuminated dial read four o'clock. Tim rolled onto his side and released his mind to sleep's anesthesia.

CHAPTER 18

▼

Tim woke to the sound of the toilet flushing. He rolled out of bed, banging his shin on the nightstand. "Shit!" he exclaimed.

Jan popped his head out of the bathroom laughing.

"Excuse me. Do you think you could put a lid on the language?"

"I'll put a lid on you!"

Tim made a failed attempt at grabbing Jan as the door closed.

Jan fumbled for the lock, but there wasn't one.

"Yikes!" he yelled, retreating into the shower stall.

"Come on out. You're safe for the moment," Tim said.

"Promise?"

"Promises are the counterfeit currency we extort from one another for safety's sake. But yes, I promise," Tim said.

Jan went to the sink to finish brushing his teeth. Tim stood behind him, wrapping his arms around Jan's slender body. He pressed his morning erection into the teen's soft butt and thought dirty thoughts. Jan blushed. He still wasn't used to this yet.

Tim looked down and mumbled, "Ugh. I've got to get rid of this!"

He moved to the toilet and began to pee.

Jan beat a discreet exit.

Mrs. Santos was putting cereal into bowls when Jan arrived in the kitchen.

"Good morning, Mrs. Santos," he greeted her brightly.

"Good morning, *Señor* Jan. Did you sleep well?"

"Yes, thanks. Is this the coffee you said you'd bring me?"

"*Sí*, let me make it the way we do for little ones in Chile."

Jan was presented with a hot mug of half coffee and half milk with a generous helping of sugar.

"Try this. If you don't like it, then perhaps coffee is not your cup of tea." She giggled at her little joke.

"Mmmm!" Jan said. "This stuff is like candy with a kick!"

Tim sauntered in. Mrs. Santos poured a cup of coffee for him.

"*Señor* Tim, your office called. They asked me to tell you that the meeting with the World Court will begin on Monday in Brussels."

"That's just four days away. Brussels, eh? I wonder why the change in venue."

"Are you leaving?" Jan said anxiously.

Tim didn't reply right away, then said, "Jan, I need to go to work for part of the day."

"What should I do while you're gone?"

"Well, there's laundry to do. Remember what I said about Mrs. Santos not doing laundry? It's like this, she either cooks for us or she does laundry but not both. I can't cook. The choice is easy."

"Laundry it is," Jan said.

"Come. I will show you how to run the machine," Mrs. Santos said.

They took off down the hall to the small bathroom that held the stacked appliances. Jan had worked the dryer before but didn't want to explain that.

Tim went into his office and logged onto the Internet. Using a secure pass-code he accessed the last updated file on Slobodan Milosovic, one time despot now on trial for "crimes against humanity and waging wars of aggression."

He read the witness list and compared it with a specific charge and found the name he was looking for. Denda Zarin, now living in Budapest, claimed to have been eye-witness to the massacre in the Kosovo village of Cuska. Tim's name was noted in brackets beside that of the witness. Mrs. Zarin had agreed to dictate a deposition for the High Court. She had agreed too, that if necessary, she would appear in person to give evidence. Tim's job was to assure her testimony in any event.

Hansford Ward was already in Cuska reconciling what was known to have happened there with Mrs. Zarin's statements. Tim would decide if she would prove a credible witness.

His fee for this kind of court activity was high, very high. His clients were wealthy men and women who were interested justice but also in ruining Milosovic as a force in the Serb world. Tyrants have a way of resurrecting themselves if they are not kept securely buried for a very long time. Tim wasn't interested in their motives, just their money. Clients paid his fees because he never got the evidence wrong. If it was there, he would get at the truth. His reputation and that of his Templars law firm was world-renowned. Every associate worked hard and to the highest standards. Personal ambition and in fighting was put aside in favor of the clients needs. The legal teams Tim had at his disposal made his work the most effective on the planet. Nobody did it better.

Tim's offices occupied part of an eighteenth century building on Rittenhouse Square. A weathered bronze plaque above the door informed interested parties that these were the offices of the Templars of Law. The company employed legal eagles world-wide who act as advocates for the princes and paupers of mankind; at least to those who run afoul of some law somewhere in the world.

Money did not determine the quality of service. Princes paid through the nose for advice and legal wrangling. Paupers paid what they could afford; usually nothing, paupers being, well, paupers. No one complained.

Since it's inception in nineteen-twenty, the firm had been the sole property of one man and that man always lived in the thirteenth floor at the Saint Roi. Currently that one man is Timothy Harold Morris. His successor would be determined on his death. Death being requisite to passing the firm on; retirement didn't count.

Tim walked four blocks to Rittenhouse Square and his office building, a registered historical site, entering through the same portal that had admitted the likes of George Washington, Thomas Jefferson, and John Quincy Adams. He summoned his assistant, Marsha Betterman, via intercom.

Always in a rush that left her out of breath, Marsha arrived with a sheaf of documents for Tim to sign as well as bonus checks for three of his attorneys. He scanned the papers, and then said, "Marsha, I'll need a ticket for tomorrow on the Concorde. Please ask Don to get the plane ready for the jump to JFK. Send my trunk ahead now."

The trunk was one kept ready at all times. It contained every imaginable item Tim would need, each suitable to his destination, whether that might be Buckingham Palace, a shooting party in the Loire Valley or even the hot sands of the Kalahari Desert.

"I'll be away for at least three weeks, perhaps more."

"Anything else?" Marsha asked.

"See if you can get Pat Hunter to meet me at the Adelphia Tavern in an hour."

CHAPTER 19

▼

The Adelphia Tavern was quiet in the early afternoon. The noonday crowd had headed back to work and Happy Hour was yet to begin. Tim had downed a martini by the time Hunter arrived.

"What's up, Tim?" he asked.

"Pat, I've got to go to Europe for a few weeks. I need someone to look after Jan until I get back. You know, keep him under your wing."

Pat said, "I can do that. We didn't get a chance to talk much last night. So what's going on with you and this kid?"

Tim laid out the whole story. "It's my intention to groom him to succeed me."

Pat was one of a few who knew anything about the occupants of the Saint Roi's thirteenth floor penthouse and their behind the scenes work.

Pat looked at Tim for a long time. "You miss Peter very much, don't you?"

In Philadelphia, his friends simply knew him as Peter de Main. In France, he was Pierre Henri de Main, Duc du Guyencourt and Compte de Nive. For ten years, he had been Tim's lover, mentor, companion and salvation, not always in that order. When he died in his sleep of a heart attack, he left Tim a fortune in cash, art, and property on three continents. By then, Peter had explained to Tim his role in the secret society known as Mundus. With Peter as his guide, Tim was initiated into the special powers of the ancient society and the mystique of the Saint Roi's thirteenth floor penthouse. Very few people knew of the power and responsibility that went with that special space. These precious few were all that remained of Mundus' elite core. Peter de Main was one, and now Tim would follow him in the tradition that spanned a millennium.

Peter was fifty-five when he picked Tim off the street in front of the condominium building. Tim was sixteen at the time and had been living in a row house in the Little Poland section of the city with a young man named Wil Luncki. The price Wil extorted from Tim for saving him from a homeless life was to pimp him to the dock workers at the nearby Philadelphia shipyard. Some of these men were closet gays. Others were straight men who got off abusing kids, and still others were frustrated married men whose wives had long since denied them the pleasures of their beds.

Tim's only friend, until he met Peter, was a Scottie dog that one of his so-called clients had left behind in lieu of payment. He had named the dog Fate. Wil was furious and threatened to kill the dog. That threat made Tim decide to take off as soon as he could. After he had stashed away enough money to make it to New York City, Tim fled with the dog under his arm.

"Well Fate," Tim said. "We're off to see the wizard!"

As it turned out the wizard was not as far way as Tim expected. Master and dog were passing the Saint Roi's front doors when Peter walked out on to Van Wyck Street. For reasons never understood, Fate began barking at Peter. Tim intervened, and the rest, as they say, is history.

When Peter died, Tim was out of his mind with grief. At the funeral he had said repeatedly, "I thought we'd have more time."

Everyone who knew and admired Peter had flown in for the service at his family estate at Bois du Fossé near Arles. The cardinal archbishop of Arles offered the Requiem Mass. Tim surprised everyone who made the trip by reimbursing their expenses.

Tim looked at Pat and sighed deeply. "I miss him a great deal." He looked off. "I've drowned myself in work for the last eleven years but now it's time to begin the process again and if Jan's the one, then I'm not going to rob him and myself of a life by waiting. I want more than ten years of loving."

"Seems reasonable, but what about the age difference? The kid's barely legal."

"I wasn't legal when I met Peter. Besides, age of consent laws are purely cultural. What's acceptable in one country is not in another and vice versa. The law merely states what a certain locale sees as prudent. You know that as well as I do."

"Okay! Okay! I'm on your side; remember? So what do you want me to do?" Pat asked.

"Just stay overnight. Mrs. Santos will be there during the day. I'm not sure when I'll be back in town."

"That's no problem. I can get the bar set up for the night and let one of the other bartenders take over. Most of them have been dying for my job anyway. Let them see what real work's like for a change."

The two men sealed the agreement with a handshake and left the Adelphia.

Tim called ahead to the apartment, asking Mrs. Santos to get a small carry-on bag ready for his trip. He arrived a few minutes later to a frantic housekeeper.

"You'd better go talk to *Señor* Jan. He's in the bedroom and is very upset," she said.

CHAPTER 20

▼

He found Jan sitting in the velvet-covered chair by the window. Before he could say a word Jan flew into his arms.

"What's all this?" Tim said softly.

"Please don't leave me," Jan whispered. It was almost like a prayer.

"I'll be back before you know it."

Jan repeated his plea. "Please don't. Please."

He began to cry.

"Aren't you overdoing it a bit?" Tim asked.

"How can you say that? You think you can turn my life upside down, buy me some clothes and then take a hike, leaving me alone? How am I supposed to live here? I don't know where I fit in yet. It's not fair and you know it. Mrs. Santos agrees with me too!"

"Mrs. Santos, eh? I might have known she'd be in on this. Stay here."

Tim found Mrs. Santos in the living room having her afternoon tea.

"Comfortable?" Tim asked acidly. "Just who's in charge here?"

"If you leave him at this stage, he won't be here when you get back. Guaranteed," she replied, with a nod for emphasis.

Tim looked at the woman, who had gotten him through more tough times than he could count. He took a deep breath, counted to ten and thought about what she had said.

"You're right, as usual," he agreed. "Pack a bag for him. I'll see what I can do. No promises though."

"I did that already. Now may I finish my tea?"

Tim nodded and returned to the bedroom and went straight to the phone. He checked his watch. Three o'clock—just enough time. Jan watched in silence as Tim dialed the number of Mason Tull, head of the Philadelphia passport office.

Years before, Tull had been wrongly accused of murdering his wife and son when they drowned in a canoe accident on the Brandywine River. The investigation was botched due to infighting between two state police agencies, and Tull's innocence was lost in the shuffle. Tull had been robbed of his job and self worth by media coverage surrounding the case. Alcohol abuse made the downward spiral of a good man a certainty. Then Tim came to his rescue and won his case in court. Tull was and would be forever grateful.

A woman with a weary sound to her voice answered at the passport office.

"Mason Tull, please," Tim said.

"Who may I say is calling?"

"Tim Morris."

Mason answered the phone quickly. "Tim! What can I do for you?"

"I know you guys close soon, but I need a favor."

"Name it."

"I need an emergency passport for today."

"You don't want much do you, old buddy?"

"I have a meeting at the World Court and am taking someone with me."

"The World Court, eh? Well, we can't hold up the wheels of justice," Tull said sourly. "Give me the details, and I'll take the passport photo myself. Try to get here soon, 'cause I have a date tonight. Okay?"

Tim gave the vital statistics. At the birth date, he let out a breath but said nothing. "That's all I need. See you ASAP!"

Tim reached out and took Jan in his arms. Jan returned the embrace with a trembling sigh.

"Well, Little Grasshopper," Tim mocked. "Are you ready to see something of Europe?"

On the way to the passport agency, Tim called Marsha and asked her to book an additional ticket for the Concorde in the name of Jan C. Phillips.

"Who's Jan Phillips?" she asked.

"I'll tell you later. Thanks, Marsha"

Marsha's return call confirmed that two tickets would be waiting for him when he got to JFK. Tim rang off before she could ask for more information on Jan.

They arrived at the Customs House on Chestnut Street with twenty minutes to spare. Mason gave Jan a quick glance before he had him pose for the passport photo. If he had any thoughts about what the relationship was between Tim and Jan he kept them to himself. This was business, and Tim's firm would pay well for the service.

Jan, who had never seen a passport, didn't notice the diplomatic cover for the document, but Tim did.

"Nice touch. Thanks, Mason," he said.

The three shook hands and left the office together. A brisk autumn wind pushed fallen leaves around the courtyard of the historic building, making a sound like little castanets.

"My date said she wanted to have a picnic tonight. I hope she meant in front of a fireplace with soft music and not a stroll in the park. This wind is getting nasty," Mason said as he moved off.

Jan shivered. "What did he mean about the passport cover?"

"It's a diplomatic passport. All it really means is, if you run into the law they can deport you but can't jail you. We'll make sure that doesn't happen," Tim said.

As they walked back to the Saint Roi, Tim dialed Pat Hunter to let him know about the change of plans.

"We leave tomorrow."

"What about my clothes?" Jan asked.

"I'll send for them. If they need any more alteration we can find a tailor in Brussels." Tim said.

Europe! Suddenly colored graphics on a paper map was going to be a reality. Jan was overwhelmed.

"I can't believe this is happening."

"Believe it." Tim answered.

CHAPTER 21

▼

Don Fisher flew covert missions for the CIA during the '70s. After his retirement from the "company," he hired on as chief flight officer for the Templars of Law. The global nature of their work kept the pilot very busy.

Fisher met Tim and Jan at a private hangar. Small jet planes were parked in the metal Quonset hut in gleaming readiness. Jan thought they looked like flying cigarettes. A man of few words, Fisher neither offered nor invited conversation. That suited Jan since he was tired and happy that he didn't have to make nice to the man. Tim too was anxious to get to JFK and on to the international terminal and so he was in no mood for chitchat either. Also, he wanted to look over the report Hansford Ward had faxed just before they left the Saint Roi.

Jan had never flown before so this first flight was a nervous time for him.

"At least we cleared the Delaware River!" he said with relief.

"Planes don't end up in the drink here. You're thinking of Logan Airport in Boston. They've had a few dippers there," Tim replied.

"Do you fly to Boston?" Jan asked

"Yep, all the time."

Jan groaned and looked out the window. By the time they had landed and gotten to the international terminal, Jan was looking decidedly green.

Tim handed him a pill. "Take this. It may help you feel better."

"How did you know I was feeling bad?" Jan asked.

"You look it."

The wait to board was an hour and ten minutes. By then Jan had regained his balance and his color. Looking at a huge painting of the supersonic aircraft, Jan wondered if it could really fly.

"It looks like the front is going to fall off!"

As they entered the passenger ramp leading to the Concorde, the sounds of the airport were muffled to near silence.

Jan turned to Tim, whispering, "This is too creepy!"

Tim chuckled. "I know what you mean. The first time I rode this beast I was terrified."

"Really?"

"Sure. Do I look like, James Bond?"

Jan smiled. "It's beginning to seem more and more like you are."

"I only use the Concorde if I have to be in Europe in a hurry. Usually, I take standard aircraft. Six or so hours in a first class seat beats riding on a buckboard any day! You'll see what I mean," Tim said.

Jan had no idea what to expect when he stepped into the passenger cabin of the SST. The aisle was narrow and seemed to stretch right out the rear of the plane. The seats, also quite narrow, were not all that comfortable. Little time was wasted in getting everyone settled in for the exit and take-off.

"I'm sweating," Jan told Tim.

"It's hot in here right now, but when we get moving the air will get cooler," Tim assured him.

No sooner had he spoken than the great plane moved away from the terminal and began to taxi across the tarmac. By the time the attendants finished their safety orientation and took their seats, the plane had reached the runway. In a roar that could shake heaven itself, the white dart zoomed skyward.

It wasn't long before a steward appeared offering a drinks menu. Tim asked for red wine. Jan opted for ginger ale.

"You're awfully quiet," Tim said.

"I'm scared shi…I'm a little nervous. Is it always this loud? I though it would be real quiet."

"Most people are surprised at how high the noise level is in any plane. I hate these seats even if they are leather. Planes always feel cramped to me."

Jan looked out the window for the first time. "Wow! What happened to the ground?"

Tim looked over. "Take a good look. This is the closest you'll ever get to God this side of heaven."

The attendant showed up a little later with their drinks. He slid a tray of breads, crackers and condiments on the pull down tables and bid Jan a cheerful *bon appetite*. Picking up a jar of what looked like jam gone bad, he looked over at Tim with a quizzical expression. "What's this stuff?"

"It's pâté."

"But what is it?"

"Goose liver that's been pureed. Port wine is added for flavor. Taste it."

"Taste it! It looks like something I've already tasted."

"That's not funny. If you don't want it then leave it. Try the caviar—the black stuff."

"Caviar. Fish eggs, right?"

"Right."

"Too bad I'm not on a diet," Jan observed.

Jan spread a thin layer of pâté on a cracker, closed his eyes and bit down on the tidbit.

"This isn't bad!"

Tim rolled his eyes in response.

Jan ate like a man on death row. Slipping into a doze he murmured, "I was hungry."

Tim finished reading the report Hansford Ward had faxed earlier. It was complete in every regard, and yet....

CHAPTER 22

▼

The Paris morning came too quickly for Tim. Jan woke him with a shake. Tim tried to remember where he was. De Gaul Airport to the hotel was a blur.

"Ugh, Jan. What time is it?"

"It's daylight. Where's your watch?"

Tim looked around. "Oh...I'm wearing it. It's six thirty. We'd better get moving."

Tim grabbed the hotel in-house phone and asked the desk to make two first class reservations on the TGF high-speed train to Brussels.

Jan headed toward the shower teasing, "Catch me if you can!"

Tim caught him with ease.

An hour later, they walked one block to the Seine. A light mist swirled up from the dark water. The sights of Paris awed Jan. "Oh my God, Tim! Look! It's Notre Dame Cathedral!"

"Come on! Come on!" Jan yelled as he ran to the river.

After breakfast, they taxied to the Gare Du Nord train station, boarding the high-speed rail for Belgium. The broad avenues of Napoleon's imperial city gave way to flat countryside. Fallow fields dotted with mini lakes stretched as far as the eye could see.

"Looking out the window makes my stomach upset," Jan complained.

"It's the speed. Try looking at an angle instead of straight out. Your eyes won't have to work so much to take in the view."

"Hey, that works!"

"Yep." Tim settled in for a snooze.

Four hours later in Brussels, they booked into the Hotel Charlemagne.

"Jan, I'll be in meetings the rest of the day and all day tomorrow. The people I have to see traveled from Bruges so we won't have to go to Holland after all. It's too bad really. Bruges is beautiful. The canals are full of swans."

"I know," said Jan. "The people of the town were forced to keep the swans there as a constant reminder of their disobedience to the emperor."

"Know it all," Tim joked. "I've arranged for you to have tours of the city. May I suggest sending Mrs. Santos a nice box of chocolates?"

"Can't I stay in the hotel?"

"I'd like it if you saw something of the place. We won't be coming back, and Brussels is one of the most important cities in Europe."

"Oh, all right." Jan pouted. "But it won't be much fun without you."

The two days passed in a blur of stuffy museums, fast trains, a glittering concert, and no sex. Jan began to wonder more and more about Tim's recent lack of desire. He was relieved and disappointed at the same time. His feelings for Time were evolving but he was still confused about their arrangement. Was this the life he was going to live? Had the dynamics of their relationship changed?

CHAPTER 23

▼

Budapest is one of those European cities that seem to be a movie set rather than a living community. Even the new buildings look old. A visitor could easily imagine it devoid of people soon after the director yells, "Cut and print!"

A heavy downpour had obliterated the midday sun. Out of sight, the blare of a police siren made Jan shiver. Tim explained the sound is intended to intimidate, and at least in this case, it succeeded. Protected by the oversized black umbrellas provided by the hotel concierge, they decided to walk the seven blocks to the address Denda Zarin had listed as her home. They walked in silence as large rain drops drummed an ominous tattoo on the stretched umbrella cloth. The bright yellow stuccoed buildings that lined the streets seemed dulled by the slanting rain. Their footfalls echoed around the narrow wet streets; made empty by the pelting water.

After a few wrong turns Jan and Tim arrived at an apartment block that looked ready for demolition. Tim found Denda's printed name tacked on the wall beside a rusty speaker grille. A button, once painted red, jutted from the splintered oak frame. Tim wondered aloud if it worked. He pressed and waited. Jan shifted nervously.

"*Qui est là?*" a woman asked in French.

"I'm Tim Morris. I wish to speak with Denda Zarin."

There was a long pause. Tim was about to ring again when the speaker squawked.

"Yes, I will open for you," she replied.

The buzzer sounded and the oak door swung open. The hall was in dim shadow. A naked bulb suspended from a frayed cord was the only illumination.

Jan drew back. "I don't like this place."

Pushing past him, Tim said, "Come on. What could happen?"

The apartment was the last unit at the rear of the ground floor. Denda Zarin opened a scarred door just as Tim and Jan approached.

She was a youngish woman. Her regular features were completely unremarkable. She wasn't fat, skinny, tall, short, pretty or plain. She was just the kind of person you might see on a street but not be able to describe later.

"Who is this?" she demanded, eyeing Jan with hostility and suspicion.

"His name is Jan. He's here to observe how I work," Tim answered.

"He was not in the agreement. He must leave, now."

Jan started to back away, but Tim grabbed his arm and brought him closer. "He stays."

Denda hesitated as if she intended to argue the point. She arched her eyebrows then shrugged and led them inside her small studio apartment. Two narrow French doors on the far right wall were ajar, leading to what Tim took to be a bathroom. A battered sofa with ripped fabric occupied the left wall facing the doors. The wall opposite the front door featured a small copper sink and a tiny two-burner stove in the corner. In the middle of this wall a short chest of drawers squatted under a dirty window; the glass cloudy and pitted from age. A rickety gate-legged table occupied the center; one leaf propped open to accommodate a single ladder-back chair.

A threadbare rug was the only attempt to hide warped floorboards. The requisite end table with reading lamp completed the ensemble. Peeling paint and general grime gave the feeling of faded elegance or shabby chic gone wrong.

The woman turned her back and moved to the chest of drawers.

"Very well. What is it you want to know?"

"Let me get my report and we can go over it together," Tim said.

He pulled out the ladder back chair and sat at the table, opening his satchel. As he pulled out papers, Jan suddenly shouted, "Look out! She's got a gun!"

They never figured out why Denda hesitated. Perhaps she didn't expect Jan to shout. Whatever the reason, that slight pause saved their lives.

Tim flung his satchel at their assailant, forcing her to duck away. That was just enough time for Tim to leap at her. Using a kick-boxer's move, he swung his leg out and caught Denda in the side. Jan heard her ribs crack.

A bone shard had punched a hole in one of her lungs. Wild with rage, the woman spat out blood and curses. She fired once. The noise bounced around the mini-room like a sonic boom. The bullet glanced the side of Tim's head just above his left ear before burying itself in the ceiling. He crashed down, pushing the only lamp in the room to the floor and smashing the bulb. Now only faint light came through the lone window's pitted glass. Everything was inky and dark. Jan's breathing was ragged with fear. His mouth was muddy with plaster dust that showered in a fine mist from the broken ceiling.

Her targets temporarily obscured, Denda groaned and bent over in pain. She sucked in a mixture of air, dust, and blood into her one working lung. Wiping her eyes with the back of her gun hand, she scanned the room looking for Tim. She saw Jan instead. Her eyes widened with fury. She grabbed her right wrist with her left hand to steady her aim.

Suddenly, Jan was knocked to the floor from behind. He coughed and shook his head and looked around. At first he thought Tim had pushed him down but then he realized Tim was lying unconscious beside him! He shook Tim's shoulder. Nothing! Fear gripped Jan's heart and he held his breath. He felt like he was going to vomit. He looked up through the table legs. A big man he had never seen before was wrestling with the woman. The two combatants twisted around the tiny room like drugged ballet dancers, legs trained as weapons tangled to gain advantage. Bits of plaster flew up from the floor in a pale film while each enemy struggled to bring the other down. The thin rug muffled their struggle. Jan could hear the woman labor for air as she tried to free herself from the big man's hold.

Finally, the man was able to get behind her. Using one hand he pinned Denda's arm back between her shoulder blades. Jerking upward, he broke it with a satisfied grunt. She went limp with a whimper. Jan heard the gun fall with a thump onto the carpet. A moment passed. He shook Tim but again there was no response. He didn't know what to do—play dead—reach for the gun—cry—run for help? In a way, help had already arrived but Jan didn't know if this man would kill all of them or not.

Jan looked up through the table legs again. For the first time he got a good look at his deliverer. Square was Jan's first impression. The man had a square head with a square haircut, square shoulders accentuated by padding in his suit coat. He may have had square hips too but he couldn't be sure since Denda's body blocked his view. The man's crumpled suit gave the impression of an unmade bed.

The big man continued to prop Denda from behind with one arm across her neck and the other still twisting the one he had just broken. She looked like a ghost as the blood drained from her face.

Their rescuer looked down at Jan and spoke in a heavy accent.

"Stand up boy. What's your name?"

Jan stood on wobbly legs.

"Jan," he replied.

"*Jan?* That's a Dutch name. Where are you from?"

Jan raised his head looking the big guy in the eye and with some pride answered, "America."

The man eyed Jan up and down.

"America, huh? I have been there. It's a nice place to visit but—"

Using the distraction of their conversation, Denda made one last effort to get free. With a backward thrust, she tried to shove the big man off balance.

What followed seemed to play out in slow motion. The man let a knife slip from his coat sleeve into his hand. He didn't even look at her as he drew the razor sharp blade across the woman's throat. Her protest was drowned in a bloody gurgle as blood sprayed in a red arc hitting Jan just below his waist. The dying woman flopped in a sloppy pile on the floor.

Jan's eyes fluttered. His knees gave way and he began to slump to the floor. The big man stepped over the woman, caught Jan and eased him onto the sofa.

It was dark by the time Tim regained his senses. His hair was matted with blood and plaster. He ached.

Well if I hurt, I must be alive…. Jan!

Tim lifted himself on one elbow and looked around. Jan was lying on the sofa. Moving on hands and knees he crawled around. He saw Denda lying on her back. Her eyes stared out unseeing. She was covered in a layer of gray plaster dust. A large tear had eroded a pasty trail across her cheek. Tim was confused. Jan couldn't have done this! He reached out for the edge of the sofa to touch the teen's throat for a pulse.

"Alive! Thank God. I've got to get you out of here!" he said.

"He's alright."

The voice from behind him thundered in Tim's sore ears. He swung around. The movement made him woozy. He slid back to the floor, resting his back against the sofa. Looking through a blue haze of cigarette smoke, he saw a man sitting at the table smoking and eating a piece of cherry pie. Tim coughed, spat and rubbed his eyes. Was he seeing things? He recognized the man as an Israeli spy.

"Joachim Nusbaum? What's Israeli intelligence doing here? Why have you killed my star witness! I assume you are responsible for this mayhem?" Wrinkling his nose he added, "And how the hell can you sit there and eat that with Madame Zarin oozing out her life at your feet?"

"That's a fine way to address your savior."

"I'll give thanks after you've answered me," Tim said.

"Very well then, I will answer your nosy questions, as far as I am allowed," Nusbaum said. "I am retired from the Intelligence Service as of last May. I killed the lady in question because she was a holdover from Milosovic's Red Beret secret police. You know the type, antisocial individuals so useful to despots who require the services of killers with extreme psychosis. Their manifesto is based in hero worship rather than ideology. They are feted, petted and otherwise pampered into believing their masters care about them. These kinds of people are very handy in some circumstances; like guarding a border. Police states routinely scour mental hospitals for violent criminals, even today. They are very adept at cultivating entire societies of these sadistic fellows."

Nusbaum took a long drag on his Turkish oval cigarette. He looked down gesturing toward the stiffening corps.

"Her real name is, or rather was, Velka Moldine. Her job was to make sure anyone prosecuting her favorite dictator got dead…very dead and very soon. The Hague judges are exempted from being hit since the parties in question feel their case is stronger if Mister Serbia himself has no credible, i.e. live accusers.…you know, people like you and your little friend over there. Oh and by the way, may I ask what in hell are you doing here?"

"I am not an accuser per se, and Jan has nothing to do with this," Tim said hotly.

"I see. He's just here for the excitement."

"Look, I came here to take a statement from the lady in question for The World Court. Jan came along because this was supposed to be a routine deposition. I sure didn't think it was going to turn deadly."

Nusbaum laughed sarcastically. "My dear friend, you did not *think* at all!"

Tim looked around. It was difficult to argue in the face of such obvious logic.

"How long…no, what time is it?" he asked.

"It's almost dawn. You two have been napping for a long time. Hungry?" Nusbaum picked up the plate and offered the last slice. "Tart?"

"How can you stand to eat with all this gore?"

He shrugged. "I worked in an abattoir while I was at university. One gets used to blood's metal odor."

"Why is a Jew running around eliminating people who kill Muslims?" Tim probed.

"A simple question deserves an equally simple answer. Genocide is genocide. It's the same for Muslims as for Jews as for Native Americans as for Africans. It's wrong. The people I work for do not make fine distinctions."

Tim looked down at the body lying between them. This couldn't be a Mundus operation or he would have known about it.

"Something I don't understand; why the throat? I thought stealth was more your style."

Joachim sighed. "This one was personal with me. I wanted her to suffer. That is all I have to say about it. As for stealth, this apartment block is scheduled for demolition. It is supposed to be empty. The woman used this place as a false address. I believe the new place will be a school for martial arts. Rather appropriate don't you think? The only person left here is an old man in the front top floor apartment. I wasn't' worried about sound. Apparently, neither was she."

"Fine, but did you have to be so messy?" Tim asked looking around the wreckage.

"You want neat? The next time you need help, call the British, they are very tidy," the ex-spy said without humor.

"So, who employs you?" Tim asked.

"I cannot answer that one, my friend. I can say that you are in danger and will remain so as long as you are here in Budapest with your young companion. I suggest you get to Italy or France where these killers have fewer contacts and so less support."

Tim dragged his satchel from under the fallen chair and searched for his cell phone. Punching in a speed-dial number he waited for an answer.

"Han," he said. "Jan and I need a complete change of clothes, underwear and shoes too. Don't ask questions, just get here as fast as you can." Tim gave the address and hung up.

"Joachim, Hansford Ward will be here in thirty minutes with our clothes. Are you alone?"

The big man just smiled. Tim was getting impatient.

"Damn it, man! I've got to get Jan out of this hell! I'm the one who's responsible if this fucks him up."

Jan spoke for the first time since the woman's murder. "I'm not fucked up, just sick, okay? And don't talk about me like I'm not here."

Nusbaum nodded towards the door and said, "My associates outside will let Mr. Ward pass without interference. Permit me to give you a piece of advice. I suggest you shower with your clothes on, then bag them and shower again. Do not forget to take the towels too. Dump them in a public container and *do* try to be discreet."

Nusbaum got up and smiled at Tim.

"You know, with a little training you could be quite good! The ribs might have killed her if you had followed up with a blow to the other side. I must go now, but I'll be back with a crew to see this place is cleaned and this mess is removed. I expect you to be gone by then, say in two hours?"

The ex-intelligence man stuffed the last piece of pie in his mouth and left quietly.

CHAPTER 24

▼

Tim sat on the edge of the sofa and stroked Jan's cheek. Jan turned and began to cry.

Cradling him in his arms, Tim said, "You're covered with blood. I'm so sorry....I didn't think....I...."

Jan struggled to get away when he saw Tim's wound and blood on his face and clothes.

"It's okay, it's okay. You're not hurt," Tim soothed.

Jan rolled into Tim's arms.

"I thought you were killed," he blubbered.

"No, I'm alright. *You're* the one I'm worried about!"

"Me! You were fantastic! Kicking that bitch like that! Where did you learn that stuff, in a martial arts school?"

"Actually no. I saw it in a Jean Claude van Damme movie. At the time it looked easy."

Jan struggled to his feet and headed for the bathroom. As he made his way around death's debris, he muttered under his breath, "So much for James Bond."

Tim staggered after Jan; his movements were jerky and his vision was blurry; he knew too, the dangers of a possible concussion. Now however, was not the time for rest and observation.

Jan moaned. "I think I'm going to be sick."

Tim turned on the shower and helped Jan into the tub. Water twirled red ribbons as Tim washed blood off Jan's clothes.

Finally, he managed to get Jan's clothes off and the blood cleaned off his skin.

"Save some soap for me," he said.

Jan nodded. "The water's not very hot."

A sound creaked from the floorboards. Tim turned and saw Han standing in the doorway.

"Don't you knock?" Tim asked.

"I thought I was invited," Han replied, feigning hurt feelings. "By the way, who's the lady asleep out there? Anybody I would know?"

"Hey, can a guy get some privacy here?" Jan said.

Tim moved Han back into the parlor.

"Where did you park the car?" he asked.

"Two streets over. There's a small plaza with some shops around it. It should be okay for a while."

"Good. When Jan finishes, take him to the car. I'll get there as soon as I get cleaned-up. Which bag is for Jan?'

"Here," Han said, handing over one of them.

Tim went back to the bathroom.

"Jan, your clean clothes are in the plastic bag. Put the wet ones in when you're dressed. I'll take care of them later."

Tim turned back to the parlor and sat for a moment at the table.

"He saved my life, Han. I was careless.... fooling with some papers and wasn't looking. If Jan hadn't seen her gun and yelled..." Tim spread his hands in a help-less gesture. "I really believe he's the one I'm looking for."

Han leaned over to inspect Tim's wound. "I hope for your sake he doesn't hold this against you. Not every kid would be so calm after what went on in here. You were lucky. This little episode could have been fatal. By the way, who did this?"

"Joachim Nusbaum," Tim replied.

"Oh, him." Han looked at the carnage. "This doesn't look like his style. Did Jan get in the way or something? The place is a wreck!"

"Oh no," Tim answered. "He intended sweetheart over there to get hurt."

"Who is she?" Han asked.

Tim filled Han in on the details, as he knew them.

"I'm ready," Jan said, standing in the doorway with a weary expression.

"Jan, You'll go with—"

"I heard the plan," Jan interrupted. "I need to talk to you for a minute Tim."

Jan closed the bathroom door behind them. He reached up and wiped the dried blood from Tim's lips before drawing him into a kiss. "I really am scared. Don't take a long time."

CHAPTER 25

▼

The rain had stopped. Cafés were opening for breakfast.

Nearing the square Han told Jan, "I want you to casually look in shop windows. I'll scan the area for anyone suspicious. When we get to the car, I'll need to check it out. Got it?"

Half an hour later they walked toward the car, parked as is European custom half in the street, half on the sidewalk. Suddenly, Han pushed Jan into an alcove, once home to a statue of a now-forgotten saint.

"I want you to stand as far back as you can. Don't look out and don't come out until I call you. If anything happens, you go straight to the American Embassy. It's in the same block as your hotel. Got it?"

Eyes wide with fright, Jan stammered, "Uhh, yeah, okay…, Han, be careful!"

Han approached the car with caution. He pulled a mirrored telescoping wand from his jacket and searched the undercarriage for explosives, then turned his attention to the engine compartment. Satisfied everything was safe, Han called Jan to the car. Just as they settled in, Tim walked up from the other direction. Jan resisted the temptation to jump into his arms.

"Everything okay?" Han asked.

"Fine. I've been thinking of how we should leave the country," Tim said.

Jan gave Tim a relieved smile but said nothing.

"Jan, did you remember to ask for your passport when you left the hotel?"

Jan patted his back pocket. "I have it here. It's a little damp."

"Good. Getting a train ticket should be no problem," Tim said.

"Where are we going?"

"Well, we won't go back to the hotel, that's for sure. I can send for our things later. The other stuff can be easily gotten along the way. We'll train to Tirana, then take a taxi to Durres on the Albanian coast. From there we can get the hydrofoil across the Adriatic to Bari, Italy. Jan, there's a hill town south of Sorrento that's heavenly. It's called Positano."

Han shot Tim a warning look.

"I know what you're thinking, but if we have people on our tail, they'll expect us to take the shortest route out and head for Trieste and across to Venice, not south through Albania. Barring any delays, I figure we should make Tirana in about ten hours. It's about three hundred and thirty miles by rail."

"Albania it is," Han said, still unconvinced.

CHAPTER 26

▼

The three boarded the train for Tirana just before nine a.m. Han had a first class compartment adjoining Tim and Jan's.

"Alone at last," Jan thought.

Tim closed the door and grabbed Jan in a bear hug.

"I'm so sorry. I had no idea this would happen. I thought this trip could make up for all the school outings you missed. It wasn't really planned that way but I thought it could be kind of a birthday present. Now—"

Jan cut in. "Whoa! I know you didn't plan it like this. I won't lie though. I'm scared. I don't like your friends, and now I'm really not so sure I want your money if it comes with all this! All this fancy stuff, I can't take it all in at once. What kind of work is it that you do that gets people killed? I was just joking when I said that you were like James Bond."

Tim led Jan to the window seat.

"Look, I'm not a spy or anything like that. Sometimes I run up against the underbelly of life, but that's just a small part of my world and what I do."

"I'm listening," Jan said. "There's got to be more. This spy stuff wasn't an accident. I may be a kid with no experience, but I didn't just fall off a turnip truck! I am educated and I know a ringer when I see one, and baby I really saw one today…or was it yesterday?"

"It was yesterday," Tim said. "Alright. I was going to wait until we got home, but I can give you an idea of what my life is about and where you fit in."

Jan sat at military attention as Tim revealed the mission of the Mundus Society and how Peter de Main recruited him to be the North American leader of the society.

"Simply put, Mundus is a global society grounded in the belief that the world can live in peace and prosperity but only when rogue individuals and states are eliminated or at least boxed in. There are six chapters, one for each continent. Antarctica is not included since it has no permanent population. There is also a chapter in Iceland. That's a nod to the oldest elected parliament in the west. I'm the head of the U.S. chapter. Some chapters elect their leader and some hand the leadership to one who is chosen and groomed for the office; either by the full membership or the leader himself. The society is not, I repeat, not democratic. Within the U.S. what I say goes. If I happen to be outside the country, I must defer to the local leader. Leaders are referred to as 'Masters'."

Jan's expression tightened with anxiety at the realization of his involvement with an organized murder.

"It's okay. I was scared I when I was chosen."

"Chosen?" Jan said shakily.

"Yes, and I've chosen you to follow me after I'm dead."

Jan sat shaking his head.

"Me? What can you be thinking? I've never heard of this outfit before. You barely know me! What if I don't want to be a part of your stupid society? Didn't what happened yesterday mean anything to you? Did you ever think to ask me about this before you included me in your plan? I had a normal life until I met you!"

"Oh, you mean the 'normal' life of a boy prostitute that you planned for yourself?"

"That's not fair! It's…it's…I don't know what it is, but it's not fair."

"The words you're looking for are emotional blackmail. And you're right, it's not fair. I'll confess, I originally wanted you for myself but then as I got to know you better, well, you seemed to be different. Smart, but more than that. You have sensitivity, an inquisitiveness that I've never seen in the other street kids I've been with. You're educated, speak well when you want to and you have an analytical mind," Tim said.

"Street kids? Are all the society members kids that got picked up off the street?"

"No, but most of the occupants of my apartment have been from the street. Their stories are in the journals in the study. When we get home I want you to read some of them. It may help you understand."

"What if I don't want to understand? What if I don't want to join?" Jan said hotly.

"Do you want out?"

Jan looked out at the rolling view trying not to cry. Finally he turned to Tim and flung himself into his arms. "You own me, body and heart. I'm bought and paid for. How can I leave?"

He looked away, then back at the man who seemed even more of a stranger to him now than when they first met.

"Tim?"

"Yeah?"

"Can I ask you something?"

"Yeah."

"You said that a lot of the guys in the apartment were street people, right?"

"That's right. The apartment dates back to the early 1900s. More than half of those who have lived there and became Masters of the society were off the street. It seems to have been a tradition but I don't know exactly why it started. It just did."

"So were you a street boy when you came to live at the Saint Roi?"

A knock at the door interrupted their conversation. Han was back from the dining car with food and drinks. Tim got another reprieve from his past.

"Food!" Jan shouted.

Han carried a tray of hardboiled eggs, cheese with crusty bread and boiled ham.

"I got Jan a beer. He certainly earned it," Han announced.

"That he did!" Tim laughed.

Jan sat and smiled in smug satisfaction.

He didn't like the beer.

After Han left to return the empty tray and bottles to the dining lounge, Tim pulled the window shade and suggested a nap before they got to Tirana. They had a long trip ahead.

CHAPTER 27

▼

They lucked out at Durres. The giant hydrofoil had begun boarding for the trip across the Adriatic Sea. A quick check of their passports was all that was needed for them to pass the security inspectors. The armed conflict in Albania had reduced tourism to a trickle, so getting a first class cabin on zero notice was no problem.

Their cabin was spacious, fitted with teak tables and built-in couches that opened to served as beds. A bowl of fresh fruit was on the desk along with a box of chocolates.

Tim made a beeline for the toilet while Jan flopped at the window.

His head was swimming. A short month had passed since his eighteenth birthday and in the last two weeks he had been swept into a world of privilege, luxury, gay sex and violence, living more in that short time than he had in all of his years before. And it was all his fault. *He* was the one who went up on Van Wyck Street, nobody forced him to go there. It was he who carried Tim's scheme to his mom. He could have kept quiet and never gone back to the tenderloin. Even in the restaurant, he could have backed out. His mom had given him one last chance but in the end he was the one who said he wanted it.

He sat quietly staring out the window as the big craft maneuvered away from the dock, making its way to open water. He thought about his mother, sisters and brother, wondering what they were doing and saying at that moment. He thought about playing chess with the old men in Minqua Park, about cloud gazing, watching a hornet catch a cicada in midair. He remembered shooting hoops with his brother Daniel. God, how he hated that game! God how he would love to play it again! If only he could go back to being a nobody from Philadelphia…if only. Jan curled into a ball and cried.

Tim started to say something about going up to find Han but decided not to intrude on Jan and his thoughts. Leaving him, Tim went to the observation deck, where he found Han standing at the portside railing. The hydrofoil had just made its transition to skimming speed.

"Where's our hero?" Han asked.

"Below, crying his eyes out."

"Don't be too discouraged, Tim. Remember how you felt when you were told that you had been given the opportunity to change your life and the lives of millions of others, people who would never know or even care that Timothy Morris ever existed?"

"Of course I do. There's one difference though. I was tougher. All my tears were cried out long before I met Peter de Main. But I was scared I'd let everyone down. I felt like had the world on my shoulders."

"But you didn't let anyone down, least of all the millions of people you didn't know and who didn't even know you existed or what you'd done for them…and neither will Jan. He is just a kid, but he's no dummy. He'll learn fast. Besides, he's three years older than you were when Peter, uhh, discovered you."

"Han, you've been a good friend as well as an employee. I hope you will be the same to Jan."

"I like him well enough. He's too young for me to be pals with. You understand."

Han looked down at the water spewing from under the boat's raised foils. "There is one other thing. His mother. How would you feel if I see her from time to time?"

Tim was totally surprised by the question. "I don't know. I'll have to think about this and what it may mean in the larger scope of things."

"Let me know what you decide before we split up in Bari." Tim nodded and left the big man. It was close to midnight when Tim returned to the cabin. Jan had stripped and was laid out in the shadowy light. He glowed like a porcelain figure resting in a velvet box.

Tim resisted the desire to take him then and there.

"Easy big fella," he joked at the stirring in his loins.

Tim undressed and slipped into the bed. Jan didn't move a muscle.

CHAPTER 28

▼

Jan woke up around dawn. The incessant throb of the massive hydrofoil engines that had lulled him to sleep, now made sleep impossible. He looked at Tim snoring like a satisfied walrus.

"How can I get out of this?" he wondered. "Do I really want to?" He slipped out of the warm bed and headed for the bathroom.

Tim reached across the bed. "Jan? Jan!"

"I'm here. I had to go to the bathroom."

"Oh, I got scared for a minute. I'm beginning to get used to having you close by."

"What time is it?

Jan checked Tim's Cartier watch. "It's five thirty."

"We still have some time. Come here and keep me company."

Jan slipped under the sheet and into Tim's arms. Any doubts he had were banished, at least for the moment. Kissing Tim with a passion he truly felt, Jan murmured, "Being in like doesn't describe how I feel about you anymore."

Tim searched for a reply, found none and contented them both with kisses.

Han rapped on their door at seven. Jan pulled on his jeans and opened the door.

"We'll be docking in about two hours. I called ahead for a car. How about some breakfast topside?"

"Han, you read my mind!"

"You two go on ahead. I need a shower first," Tim called out. He hoped Jan would become more comfortable with Han, especially if the man was going to date his mother.

By the time Tim joined them, Italy's coast was a pencil line on the shimmering water.

"Looks like we'll be arriving sooner than I expected," Tim said, nodding to the horizon.

Jan stood to leave the two men. "I'll get my shower now."

"Okay," Tim said.

As Jan walked away, Tim asked Han, "Is he alright? I mean, did he say anything?"

"No, but there's got to be some fallout from the killing. And I think he's sorting out his feelings for you but he may not be too sure how you feel about him."

"Is that a clinical observation or your gut reaction?"

"I've seen just about every kind of human emotion in almost every situation. Sure looks like he's going through some real shit. It's up to you to keep him on course. If you're not feeling what he's feeling you've got to level with him."

"You're right, of course. This assassination thing simply wasn't supposed to happen. Damn it, Han, I had no idea we were in danger. Although, the report you faxed me was too perfect..., know what I mean?"

"Not really, I just get the information. It's your job to figure out what it means."

"I spoke with Joachim Nusbaum this morning," Han said, patting the cell phone in his pocket.

"How the hell did you get through to him?" Tim asked.

"It's my job to do that sort of thing. Anyway, they erased our trail and purged Denda, I mean Velka's files so that no record of you or Jan will be found. It seems our girl was working freelance and was sloppy in communicating just who her target was. Bottom line you're home free."

Tim whistled. "That's a load off my mind. I'll tell Jan too."

Italy seemed much closer that the last time Tim looked. "Reckon we be another hour off?" he asked, slipping back to the mountain patois of his youth.

"More like two. You know how deceptive distances are on the water."

CHAPTER 29

▼

Cars, buses, trucks, and pedestrians swarm around the docks of Bari in the kind of organized chaos that is Italy.

Han had arranged an Alfa Romeo for Tim. As they neared the car, Tim took Han aside. "I've been thinking about you and Joy Phillips. I can't see why you two can't see one another."

"I didn't expect any objections, but I needed to be sure. After all you're the boss. Oh, by the way, I went on the Internet and got driving directions to Paestum. You can pick up the Amalfi coast road west to Positano. Also, even if you stop for lunch at Paestum you can still make Positano by five o'clock."

"Thanks for running interference for me."

"Wait until you see my fee for all this hand holding," Han laughed.

Tim signed the rental papers for the car while Jan and Han said their farewells.

"Where's Han going now?" Jan asked.

"Back to Philadelphia. There's work for him with another outfit. He stayed here longer than he expected."

Map in hand, Jan navigated Tim through the city and out on to the main highway west to Paestum.

"Hey!" cried Jan. "That sign says Brindisi! That's where Crassus defeated Spartacus and the rebel slave army. My last year at Saint Dom's we read Tacitus' account of the battle, in Latin of course." His voice trailed off in a fit of memory.

Tim reached over and squeezed Jan's thigh.

"It's okay to think about your past. Emotions that you try to suppress always come back to haunt you in hideous forms, so don't bury your thoughts."

Jan put his head back and let his mind wander. Hours later, Tim shook him awake.

"Hey Sleepy Head. Hungry?"

"Starved! Where are we?"

"You slept almost the whole way! We're at Paestum. The best-preserved temple to Neptune is right over beyond those pine trees. It's on the edge of the cliff overlooking the sea."

The Calypso Hotel offered a picnic basket for tourists who wanted to eat by the temple. Tim and Jan opted for the tomato and fresh mozzarella plate and a bottle of semi-sweet white wine. Like the other tourists, they walked the short distance to the temple.

Jan wandered around the massive columns, feeling them, almost caressing them. Tim watched him absorb the place.

"You know, I studied the history of this place in my Latin classes. I never thought I'd see it for real. Thanks."

"I'm glad you're having a good time."

Back on the road, Jan held his safety belt in a death grip. Tim looked over and laughed. "This is the famous or should I say infamous Almalfi Drive. It was built by Napoleon's troops after he conquered the area."

"Did they make it so narrow on purpose?" Jan asked.

"Well, they didn't have cars in mind when it was built, that's for sure!"

Tim pressed the accelerator speeding though the towns of Ravello and Amalfi, finally reaching Positano just after five in the afternoon. The autumn sun was beginning to set as they entered the only car park available.

"We have a bit of a walk. All these towns are carved into the hillside. The hotel I want is right on the beach, just off the main square. It's the Buca d' Bacco…that's Bacchus' Cellar. You can just make out the sign at the bottom of the street."

"Wow! This place is beautiful!" Jan declared.

"Wait until you see the view from our room."

"Our room? How do you know what the view will be like?"

"Peter brought me here for my eighteenth birthday. That's why I wanted you to see it now."

"I see. Is this trip for me or for you?"

Tim's happy face slipped.

Jan noticed it immediately. "I'm sorry! That was harsh. I didn't mean to hurt you!"

"Forget it." Tim said flatly and picked up his pace. Jan followed in misery.

They stopped outside a pharmacy.

"Wait here, I'll be right back," Tim said.

Jan walked over to the church and peeked in. The flames of hundreds of votive candles glinted off golden cherubs that tumbled over one another in a riot of Baroque exuberance. A few minutes later, Tim came up from behind.

"Beautiful, isn't it?" he asked

"Yeah! Did you get what you needed?"

"Yep. Let's go. I want to settle in and make a reservation at La Cambusca. It's the best place in town for dinner."

Their hotel reservation for five nights confirmed, Tim and Jan took the stairs to their sixth floor suite. The sight that greeted Jan was overwhelming. Through the balcony doors was a postcard view. White-washed walls capped with red tiles formed an artificial skin for the steep escarpment that began at the water's edge and ended in misty clouds. He turned to Tim smiling and crying at the same time.

Dinner was a brief affair. Jan still felt rotten over his nasty remark earlier. Tim's return to happy conversation didn't help him with his self-reproach.

Back in their rooms Tim opened the package he had gotten at the pharmacy. "Here," he said, handing two boxes to Jan.

"What's this?"

"They're Fleet enemas."

"Enemas! Why?" Jan asked.

"You took physics in school, didn't you?"

"Yeah?"

"And what is the Law of Impenetrability?"

Jan thought a minute then answered, "No two objects can occupy the same space at the same time."

"Right. Think about it."

"Oh."

"The English instructions are on the folder inside the box. And be sure to shower when you're finished."

CHAPTER 30

▼

Tim turned all the lights off but one. Jan found him on the balcony toying with a glass of wine.

"Here. Drink this, you may need it."

Jan knew what this was leading to. His instinct was to leave but he knew that was not an option.

"Ummm....no, thanks."

Jan was nude under a terry towel. Bougainvillea and yellow trumpet vine enclosed the balcony in privacy. Tim fingered the terrycloth, tugging until it fell. Jan was still unsure; scared but also excited and physically aroused.

Tim drew a short breath. Jan's luminous skin always made him dizzy with desire.

"Did I ever look that beautiful?" He wondered.

"Cocked and ready for action, I see," Tim said with an ugly shadow in his voice.

"Yeah, this thing is a real stool-pigeon," Jan joked nervously.

"At least I know where I stand," Tim replied. "Get on your knees."

Jan nodded. Kneeling on the red terracotta tiles, he opened his mouth whispering to himself, "My first time."

Tim unzipped his pants. Jan, reached up. He was surprised at how hot Tim's skin felt. He knew what he was expected to do.

"Wait a minute," Tim said. "Let's go inside." He pushed Jan into the room and back onto the bed.

Immediately Tim was on top of him. Jan felt the warmth of his body enveloping his and started to feel more comfortable, more relaxed. He felt his sexual

being finally awaken and let himself respond with a passion equal to Tim's. Soon
he had Tim panting with lust.

Tim pulled away.

"Wait. Let's slow down a little, we don't want this to be over too soon."

Then suddenly, Tim barked, "Rollover on your knees and put your head on
the pillow.

Jan was startled by Tim's sudden mood change. He looked into Tim's determined eyes and obeyed. The soft light threw hard shadows across the walls.

"Take me!" Jan pleaded.

Tim got on the bed behind Jan and grabbed him at the waist. He thrust forward. Jan tried to pull away. He began to squirm.

"Stop! Tim it hurts! Stop!"

"No it doesn't" Tim hissed in Jan's ear.

"Please stop! It HURTS too much!"

Jan pulled and twisted. Sobbing, he fell forward clawing up toward the headboard in a frenzied attempt to escape the burning pain in his guts. Tim fell on
Jan's back caressing the taught skin.

"Easy, Jan, just lie still and breathe. Let yourself get used to it."

Speechless and covered with a fine sweaty mist, Jan merely nodded on the
verge of tears. The pain began to ease as Tim held him in a spoon hug.

"You're fine," Tim soothed. "I want this to be good for both of us. Rest now."

An hour passed. Jan roused from a fitful dream when Tim turned him onto
his right side. Jan felt the lust in Tim's finger tips as they played across his shoulder.

"Jan, just breathe easily."

"Tim, I can't do this."

"Yes you can."

"Are you ready?"

"I guess so, but please go easy."

Jan tried to match the steady rhythm of Tim's body on his. He could feel himself giving way. Just as he let himself respond to Tim's passion, Tim ordered. "I
want you on your back!"

"Like a girl? You want me like a girl?" Jan asked in disbelief.

"It's the easiest position for me. This time is for me."

"Every time's for you," Jan muttered.

"What?"

"Nothing."

Tim mounted him in one thrust. Jan gasped and thrashed his head from side to side in pain.

"Please stop!"

Ignoring Jan's plea Tim slammed into him again and again. Jan felt as if he were being attacked.

Tim growled and with a shudder, collapsed onto Jan. They lay there a while. Tim rolled off Jan and smiled. His satisfied grin was met with an angry glare.

"What's wrong?" Tim asked.

"Why did you hurt me? When I asked you before if you were going to hurt me, you said no." Jan rolled over on his side pounding the mattress. "You son of a bitch! I don't want you to ever do that to me again! I'm not a masochist! I'm not!"

Tim twisted a handful of Jan's hair.

"It's quiz time. Let's see what you've learned. Who are you?"

Jan hesitated. "Your boy."

"What is your purpose?"

"I don't know what you want me to say."

"I'll explain it in terms less subtle than I prefer. You, Jan Phillips, are a life-support system for my pleasure. If and when I change that status I'll let you know. And don't make me get rough with you again. This makes twice there won't be a third time!"

Tears rolled down Jan's face as he ran into the bathroom.

"I'm sick of feeling like I'm on a roller-coaster," he yelled back.

Jan sat on the toilet, head in hands. This can't be right! He was confused. The sex hurt but it felt good too; he was appalled at being screwed while on his back but that too felt right at the time. He wanted to please Tim but he was afraid of him at the same time. He wondered if girls felt like this too when they had sex and whether these feelings went away or changed.

When Jan didn't come out of the bathroom right away, Tim went to the balcony and looked out at the picturesque town below.

"God, why couldn't I make it good like it was with Peter?" he asked the sky.

"Because I'm not you, and you're not Peter," came a voice.

Tim turned. Jan had followed him, at a safe distance.

"Tim I want to please you, but I can't let you change the person I am, even if I am dumb and inexperienced at least I know that much." Jan sighed. "Am I making any sense?"

"Yes, not very eloquently but you are. I'm an asshole."

It seemed like Tim wanted to say more at that point but didn't.

Jan walked up to Tim and put his arms around his waist. "Can I go to sleep now?"

*   *   *   *

By morning, Jan had tied his pillow into a sailor's knot. Tim sat, his back resting against the mahogany headboard, watching the late-morning sun burn the last mists from the shore.

Jan moaned and rubbed his sore behind. Tim kissed him awake. "The day is broke, look about. Come, we've got things to do."

Tim stepped in the shower while Jan peed his morning hard-on away.

"Ugh! Can't let Randy Andy see this," he mumbled.

CHAPTER 31

▼

Positano's shops were doing a brisk business by the time Jan and Tim made their way to the central square.

"We need some clothes," Tim said.

"I know. I feel like these are going to rot off me. By the way, where's your trunk?"

"Han took care of it. He's sending the stuff we left behind to France. Your new clothes from Mr. de Silva will be there too. That's where we're heading. You know, Jan, Han is amazing. I wish I could get him to work for me full-time, but he likes variety."

Two hours later, they were decked from the skin out in new gear.

"What do we do with our old clothes?" Jan asked.

"The hotel has a laundry service."

Jan looked out at the aqua sea splashing against the basalt blocks that made up part of the fishermen's dock.

"Hey! Do you think the water's still warm enough to swim?"

"Sure. Let's get our stuff and hit the waves."

When Tim was light-hearted, Jan forgot how volatile he could be. He wondered what made Tim so unhappy.

As they lay on the volcanic rock that served as the beach, Jan asked Tim about his childhood. Tim gave out a sigh and finally told Jan about growing up in the small West Virginia town, how it felt to be cast out of his church and abandoned by his family because of his homosexual tendencies.

Thinking of his own situation now Jan asked, "Do you ever look back and wish you had stayed."

"I did for the first year. Then I met Peter, and I never had time to think about it much. Besides, they didn't even try to find me. I didn't have to be hit in the head with a brick bat to understand that I wasn't wanted."

Although a few people walked on the beach, Jan reached over and held Tim's hand.

"*I* want you."

When Tim didn't respond, Jan jumped up. "I'm going in again. Want to come along?"

"No, I'll stay here....Don't go out too far."

Tim lay back and let the sun bathe him. Once again, he surrendered himself to memory. It was autumn, and he was fourteen, walking from Little Fork to Philadelphia using a road map he had found in his father's garage. With each mile he grew more hopeful that he would be picked up by some kind driver. No such luck! He thanked God for the clear weather and a new pair of sneakers.

Four weeks later, he had reached the Philadelphia suburb of Bryn Mawr. His one and only ride came just outside the city limits. An elderly woman had turned too close to the pavement. She clipped the curb causing a blowout. Tim changed her tire and for his trouble got a ride into center city Philadelphia. He was surprised and a little disappointed that the lady didn't ask more about him and what he was doing alone on the road.

Tim had fourteen dollars and thirty-two cents in his pocket when he was dropped off on Arimingo Avenue in the heart of Philadelphia's "Little Poland." It was dark. He was lost and alone in the largest city he'd ever seen.

A broadsheet stapled to a telephone pole advertised Teresa's Polish Buffet, all you could eat for five bucks.

A thought: "Maybe I can work for food."

Using the street signs as guides Tim found Teresa's just two blocks away.

"Not bad for a start," he tried assuring himself as he walked across the parking lot.

Bracketed by a McDonald's and a local sandwich and deli shop, Teresa's held center stage in a long strip mall. Tim's mother had always cautioned her children against food loaded with chemicals and empty calories so he didn't even consider fast food. Besides, he was starved and a burger just wouldn't cut it.

The restaurant was a large, bare room with rows of Formica tables and plastic chairs. Buffet counters were arranged across the rear wall. Bright fluorescent lights added a harsh, reflected glare.

The aroma of kielbasa, cabbage and mashed potatoes made Tim's mouth water. An overly endowed middle-aged woman in black stretch pants and a red rayon top stood guard behind the cash register. Her fake red hair and fire engine red lipstick made her look like a clown.

Tim asked about working for food.

"We don't need help right now. Are you Polish?"

Tim tried to hide his disappointment. "No, I'm not," he answered.

"If you can't pay you'll have to go," she said without emotion.

"I have money, but I need a job too."

"No work here. If you want to eat it will be five dollars plus tax. All you can eat."

Tim paid her and followed the woman's instructions on finding the plates and flatware.

He was down to nine dollars.

Small signs taped to plastic sneeze guards covered the steaming trays. "Take as much as you want. Please don't waste the food," the writing instructed.

Wasting food was his last thought!

In no time he loaded his plate with every item offered. He learned that hot kielbasa was just that....hot and spicy! As he began to eat, a young man walked up to the table. He wore an apron with a nametag hooked to the bib. It read, *Wil Luncki.*

Wil, a native of Poland, was nineteen and had been in the United States for ten years. He had dirty blond hair cut short, narrow brown eyes and pale acne-scarred skin. His height was middling, but he had broad shoulders and strong hands. His voice was pleasant, almost musical.

"Have you been here before?" he asked.

"No, I just got into town today. I've never been to Philadelphia," Tim answered.

"I will be bringing your drink. Refills go with the dinner. You're supposed to leave the used plate and get a clean one for each helping. What can I get you?"

Tim considered his finances. "Water is okay for now, thanks."

"Water is in the cooler. Cups are in the rack at the end of the steam counter. What's your name?"

"Tim. What's yours?"

Wil smirked and pointed to his nametag.

Tim nodded. "I'm new here. Do you know of anybody hiring for full-time or part-time work? I need a place to stay too. Salvation Army maybe?"

"Salvation Army!" Wil laughed. "This is a strictly Catholic neighborhood. Those guys don't make out too good around here." He gave Tim a sidelong glance. "How old are you?"

"Fourteen, almost fifteen."

"I get off work in an hour. Maybe I can help you out, but no guarantees."

Tim smiled his relief. "Thanks! You're the first person I've actually talked to since I left home."

"We can talk about all that tonight. Just eat up and wait for me outside when you're done."

"Okay!" Tim said enthusiastically.

Wil lived in what was left of a block of row houses. Fire and vandalism had reduced their numbers to just seven. "I rent this dump for five hundred a month, but I get privacy and it's close to work so I don't mind the cost," Wil said as they climbed the once-white marble steps up to the steel door.

Darkness did nothing to hide the grimness. The layout was standard row house construction, set by designers of workers' houses a hundred years ago. All the rooms were rectangular with a parlor, dining room and kitchen in a long line on the ground floor. Rickety stairs led to the second floor, which originally featured three bedrooms but no bath. One had been converted to a shower, toilet and sink in the early 1930s. Leaky plumbing had made the bathroom floor mushy with rot.

Tim looked around. One bedroom was furnished. The door was removed on the other, which was stuffed with debris.

"Where will I sleep?" he wondered.

"Wil," Tim said. "I have to go to the bathroom."

"Help yourself. I'll put your duffle bag in the bedroom."

Tim sat on the toilet. Reaching up, he opened the window but the foul air was worse than the stink he was making so he shut it again.

"Mind if I shower?" he called out.

"Go ahead," came the reply.

Tim was relieved to see the shower was actually pretty clean. Soap was plentiful, and so was the hot water. Things were looking up, until he stepped out of the shower and found his clothes were gone.

He grabbed a towel, put it around his waist and ran into the bedroom. Wil had dumped his duffle bag out and was going through his pant pockets.

"What do you think you're doing? That's my private stuff!" Tim yelled.

Wil held up a hand. "Whoa there! This is my house, and I don't know you from Adam. I just wanted to make sure you don't have drugs."

"Well I don't!" Tim said angrily. "And I don't want you messing with my things."

"Keep your shirt on, or maybe I should say your towel." With that Wil yanked it off him.

"Nice! Very nice," Wil said, leering at Tim.

Tim had never compared himself with the other kids in gym class, so the observation was unexpected. At fourteen he hadn't achieved his full manhood, and yet what he had was nothing to be ashamed of.

"Your pubes will have to be shaved off, but all in all you've got a very nice package," Wil said.

Tim blushed. His voice was panicky. "What are you talking about?"

"I'm talking about that job you need. I know lots of guys who'll pay you to have sex. Some are into blowing, some want to get done and others are anal queers."

"I don't know anything about that kind of stuff!" Tim cried.

"That's what I'm here for, cutie pie. Now don't tell me you're not a homo. I spotted you right from the first."

"I...I don't know....I mean I'm not sure." Tim put his hands over his face and sat on the bed. Wil reached over and stroked Tim's thigh.

Tim turned and closed his eyes. Instead of the kiss he expected and needed, he was pushed down on the yellowed sheet. Grinning, Wil straddled Tim's face.

"Time to pay for that shower, kid," he said. "Open wide."

Tim stared up. The ripe odor of unwashed skin swept out from Wil's thighs. Tim closed his eyes and opened his mouth. His first sensation was to gag. All he could taste were salt and urine. He tried to push Wil off but he was pinned too neatly to make a getaway.

"No teeth now. I don't want to have to hurt you," his tormentor warned.

Tim tried to stretch his mouth. At last Wil gave out a grunt without warning. Tim fought for air. He pound on Wil's legs, hoping he would let him up.

"Swallow," Wil demanded. "You might as well get used to it."

Tim relaxed his throat. Wil climbed off his chest and went into the bathroom. "Ugh, I need a piss."

Tim rolled over on his side. He watched a cockroach feed on the edge of the wallpaper. Wil came in, noticed the bug, smashed it, and then fell into the bed. Tim looked at the wall a long time before he realized that the random design wasn't a pattern but squashed roaches.

"My first time," he said gently. He slept.

CHAPTER 32

▼

Tim woke with a start. Jan was dripping water over him.

"Are you okay?" Jan asked.

"Yeah, why?"

"You were sayin' stuff. I couldn't make out what."

Tim stood. "Let's go for a walk."

Narrow streets covered with lattice to shield pedestrians on hot summer days gave way to cobbled courtyards draped with fragrant vines.

Jan was often boisterous in his happiness, laughing for no reason other than just being with Tim. Neither tried to hide their delight with each other. Everyone they met was friendly, seemingly at ease with them as a couple.

"You were right, Tim. This place makes you feel all the ugliness in the world is a dream and this is reality. I wonder what it would be like to live here all the time."

"I don't think you'd like it. As trite as it may sound, there really is no place like home."

Home. Jan's thoughts turned to Kensington. He had been gone only a few weeks, but Philadelphia and Saint Dominic's seemed as if they were in another world; one that never really existed.

Evening clouds shaded the setting sun as they arrived on the hotel terrace.

"How about a drink before we go up?" Jan asked.

Tim gave him a long look. "A drink?"

"Yeah, why not?"

"Sure, why not?"

Tim introduced Jan to one of his favorite drinks, Campari on the rocks with a twist of lime. Jan wrinkled his nose.

"It tastes like grass."

"That's because it's made from herbs. Too strong?"

"Oh, no! I like it!" Jan exclaimed.

"Tim, how long did you say we'd be here?"

"A few more days. Are you anxious to leave?"

"I like it a lot. I was just wondering."

Days and nights blended in frolic and lovemaking. When they weren't exploring the surrounding hill towns of Almafi and Ravello, Tim and Jan explored their bodies. Tim fought off the imps that prodded hidden memories of humiliation, sadness, loss and above all deep, ferocious anger. In turn, Jan became less wary of Tim's passion

*   *   *   *

Heavy rain soaked them as they left the hotel for the last time. They trudged up the hill to the town's only car park. There, inside the car, Tim and Jan dried themselves and changed into dry clothes.

"We'll go to Sorrento find a ship and get passage to Marseilles or Nice," Tim said.

"How do you know all this stuff, where to get boats and trains and where they go?" Jan asked.

"A lot has to do with Peter. He lived in Europe and the U.S. so naturally we traveled. He was my mentor and introduced me to people of influence. Some of what I know comes from the work I do too. Remember I'm just Tim Morris from tiny Little Fork, West Virginia; I wasn't born knowing about the world and how it works. People have to teach that to you. If you are lucky, you get someone like Peter to help. If not, well—"

Jan shook Tim's shoulder.

"You okay?"

"Yeah, just thinking."

The rain didn't slow the hellish traffic on the narrow road. By the time they arrived at the dock in Sorrento, Tim's palms were sweating. After Jan retrieved their baggage, Tim returned the rental car.

"We have a choice," Tim announced. "We can take a windjammer schooner or a small cargo ship with passenger cabins. The schooner goes directly to Nice. The cargo ship is bound for Marseilles. Which do you prefer?"

Jan eyed the sailboat and the steady rain pelting the slick cobblestones.

"Marseilles," he said flatly.

"What, no sense of adventure?"

"Haven't we had enough of that for a while?"

"Avignon doesn't have an airport, so we would have to train from either Nice or Marseilles anyway. It's about an even draw."

"How long will it take?"

"Two days max. There's one stop at Corsica. Want to see where Napoleon was born?"

CHAPTER 33

▼

Han's plane landed in Philadelphia late in the afternoon. As soon as he arrived at this apartment in Society Hill Square, he phoned Joy Phillips. She seemed neither surprised nor unhappy that he called. Yes, she would be home tomorrow evening. The children were away at her sister's for a long weekend. Was this information an invitation? Han tried to turn the gratuitous remark around in his head, but he was too tired from the flight to consider anything deeper than his Jacuzzi.

Across town, in a world far removed from Han's posh Society Hill apartment, Joy sat looking in the mirror, smoothing back the lines around her eyes.

"What am I doing?" she thought. "He's probably coming to get stuff for Jan."

Jan, not a day passed that she didn't think of him, wonder about him and whether he was alright; hating herself for taking that perv's money. Hating her life and wondering where she would be now if she hadn't married Bill Phillips.

*　　　*　　　*　　　*

Han arrived at her door at nine p.m. the following evening. Joy's breath caught in her throat. She had forgotten how disfigured his face was.

"I hope I'm not intruding," he said.

"No. I'm just waiting for you to tell me what you want. I assume you've come for some of Jan's things."

"Not really. What I want is that cup of coffee you promised me."

"Oh...Well, yes, I can make a pot for us. I'm sorry if I sounded rude. I'm still not right with all this."

Han didn't understand how she could have agreed to Tim's demands but it really was none of his business but he was attracted to the woman. Perhaps he sensed the same survival instincts in her that he too possessed.

"Just so we don't have to tiptoe around the subject, Jan is okay. He seems to be getting along with Mr. M just fine," Han said.

"Thanks for telling me that. Am I allowed to ask any more about him?"

"No," Han answered flatly.

"How do you take your coffee?" Joy asked defeated.

"I like it blond like my women."

Joy blushed at the apparent come-on.

They talked to well after two in the morning. Han looked at his watch. "I should be going."

"Do you have to go?" Joy looked away, not wanting to stare rejection in the face.

"No, I don't *have* to go. I'll stay if that's what you want."

"It's what I want."

At six, Han left Joy with a smile and a promise to call later in the week.

CHAPTER 34

▼

Corsica, Marseilles, the walled city of Avignon, each tumbled in Jan's head in a kaleidoscope of sound, smell and sight.

They had been driving for most of the day when Jan complained that he was feeling burned out. "Can't we just stop someplace and rest? If I see one more monument to a dead person I'll barf."

"Funny you should ask. We're almost home."

"And where exactly is home?" Jan asked with barely masked sarcasm.

Tim turned the car onto a tree-lined boulevard. Autumn in the south was late this year. Tall poplars waved farewell with golden leaves to the dying sun.

Jan sat in unhappy expectation. Here wasn't his idea of home.

"Probably just another hotel with no heat," he thought.

The ocher stones and pale blue roof tiles of the chateau *d'Alene Coeur* glowed in the late afternoon. During the French Revolution, angry citizens pulled down the original mansion. Seventy-five years later Louis Napoleon, grateful for the de Main support of his regime, restored it to them.

"Don't just sit there. Don't you want to see our house?" Tim asked.

"I'm not sure. What are we doing here?"

"Peter left this house to me when he died. I thought you'd like to see it."

Tim was upset with Jan's attitude. He stormed across the cobbled courtyard and through the front doors. Jan trudged along, kicking himself for being such an ass.

"What the hell's wrong with you?" Tim asked.

"I didn't expect this. I know you're rich and all...but this!"

"What? You don't like it?"

"Like it? I don't even know what it is! Can't you get it through your head that I'm new to all of this? I'm just a guy from Kensington. What do I know about palaces?"

"Jan, you need to understand that your life has changed. As long as you keep thinking that way, you'll never be at home in the world. Besides, it's not a palace. It's just a big old house. A rather nice house at that, I might add."

"It's big alright, and I guess it's pretty. Is it really yours?"

Tim chuckled, "Do you take me for a gatecrasher? Of course it's really mine." He pulled a braided cord and a bell rang.

"Let's see if we can get somebody to feed us."

"Now you're talking!" Jan said happily.

A plump woman with a cheery smile appeared as if by magic.

"Monsieur Morris! We did not expect you until much later." She looked curiously at Jan.

"Not to worry Matilde, we are early. Permit me to introduce my friend Jan Phillips."

"*Enchanté monsieur.*"

"*C'est un plaisir Madame,*" Jan replied.

"Matilde, may we have something to eat? I know it's early but we are very hungry"

"*Oui, oui, monsieur,* Right away," she said hurrying off to tell the staff that *Le seigneur* had arrived.

Tim turned to Jan. "You're just full of surprises. First Latin, now French. I don't suppose you speak Swahili too?"

Jan laughed. "That's the all the French I know. I took Beginning French my last semester at Saint Dom's but there really wasn't much time to learn anything useful. I'm surprised I even remembered that much!"

After dinner, Jan asked Tim to explain more about the aims of the Mundus Society.

"We try to establish a balance between the stable countries and the instable ones, either through diplomacy or by influencing their economics, and sadly, in some cases, war. On rare occasions it becomes necessary to remove people from powerful positions. Killing is not an aim but can be a consequence of our activities. I am proud to say that I have never ordered a death as a means of change."

Jan pulled a long face. "Oh, come on, how can a small group of people who don't live in a particular country control it?"

"It's not always easy or even effective. The inner core of Mundus is very small but there are thousands of members in all levels of society, so we do make a difference. And we don't try and run the day-to-day activities of government or courts or the economies. But when a nation runs amok either within its own boarders or causes trouble outside of its realm, we expect institutions like the United Nations to intervene. If that doesn't happen we guide certain people to the ends we feel will give the best result for everyone.

"Take the situation in Rwanda," Tim went on. "When it became obvious that the great powers were going to stand by and let the killing go on we brought pressure to bear and turned the tide against war. It was all very behind the scenes."

Tim took a sip of wine, "But I have to confess that the motives of the society aren't always altruistic. Often it's the stability of a region that calls for action rather than the plight of the people there. Sometimes the individual is lost to the majority good. Personally, I don't like it when that happens. I believe in individual worth. I abhor a society that demeans any person. During the Renaissance, homosexual men and women were valued not for what they were but for what they brought to their cultures. And I don't mean just painters like Leonardo da Vinci. There were scientists, philosophers, engineers, and explorers. But at the same time, people were roasted alive because they disagreed with either the Pope or the emperor."

"This sounds like people controlling the whole world." Jan said disapprovingly.

"No, you're confusing Mundus with the Illuminati."

"Never heard of 'em," Jan said.

Tim laughed. "I'm not surprised. They are a secret society bent on establishing single global order through controlling the world's money supply. Mundus, on the other hand, values individual nations and the unique position each has in developing a just and safe world. I believe that the rule of law is the most effective way to accomplish goals. Not all Masters share my philosophy, but they are from different cultures and philosophies."

Jan sat trying to absorb it all.

"Whoever follows me must believe as I do or I won't appoint him or her."

"Her? There are women Masters?"

"Yes, two of them. One is Icelandic. Icelanders have their own Master. How do you think Reagan and Gorbachev ended up in Reykjavik?"

"You did that! We read about the beginnings of glasnost and perestroika in social studies. I thought Reagan was the big power behind it."

"I didn't do it personally, but I managed the team who put the ideas together."

Jan thought about what this might mean to him and his future. He wasn't sure he was up to the responsibilities.

"Tim I'm not sure about me getting involved in your club. Can't you get somebody else to join?"

"Jan, you've been through a lot in these last weeks and you've handled it like a trouper. You're made of sterner stuff than you give yourself credit for. Your warning me that the Moldine woman was going to shoot us made all the difference in our survival. I don't think that was a fluke. I was very distracted, although I had an odd sense that something just wasn't right about her…from the documents Han got for me, I mean. There I was, Mr. Joe professional all tied up in la-la land while you were the one with your wits about you. I guess love made me careless."

Tim took a deep breath. He realized that what he had just said would make or break their relationship.

"Love…? Are you saying you love me…?"

Still unsure, Tim answered cautiously, "As much as I can."

Jan's face lit up like a thousand candles. He took Tim by the hand.

"Where the hell's the bedroom in this place?"

CHAPTER 35

▼

"Jan, it'll be Christmas soon. Do you think you can get through the holidays in Philly or would you rather stay here?" Tim asked.

Jan looked out at the bleak December sky.

"I love it here. I didn't at first, but everyone is so nice. You seem happier here too. I'd like to stay, but I guess it's really up to you."

"To tell the truth I have to be back by New Year's Day," Tim said.

Jan thought of his family and the temptation to contact them.

"Let's go then."

They had used their time well at the chateau. Tim spent long hours teaching Jan the history of the Mundus Society as well as how the various chapters functioned. Each capital city had its own Master who reported in turn to the "continental" master. Jan learned the Master's names and their cities. He went alone to Paris to visit the head of the French chapter, carrying with him a ciphered letter of introduction from Tim. The report back to Tim was that Jan had been charming, quick to understand the goals set for the coming year and best of all showed a true interest in the philosophies of those members not tied to western democracies.

Tim wrapped up the final details for next year's upkeep on the chateau and the staff payroll. He went over these details with Jan as well.

As their time in Arles wound down Jan spent more and more time wandering the town alone with his thoughts. Winter, with its sudden chill, had stemmed the flow of tourists hordes. The ancient Roman amphitheater with its Latin graffiti delighted Jan. Hieroglyphs and text called out from the past, *remember me*. Some were pathetic little notes scratched on cell walls. Others were pornographic. It would seem that basic needs are not diminished by circumstance.

Two days before they were to return to the States, Jan visited a man he had become very fond of, Jacques Malreve, the Father Abbot of Saint Sebastian monastery. A monk for thirty years, Jacques had been head of the monastery for the last ten. Jan had asked the abbot to help him with conversational French. In return, the man insisted on speaking Latin with Jan.

As he explained to Jan, "It pleases me to speak once again in the language of my ordination. These young men today simply don't have the language down for conversation."

While Jan awaited him in the study, silvery light streamed through a row of windows set high in the gray stone walls. Square holes evenly spaced under them were the only remnants from the medieval defense works the monks used against attacks from marauding bandits.

Jan fingered the old texts that lined the rough walls. It was very still in the room. The crack of an ember drew his attention to the fireplace. He had looked at it often when he and the abbot were together but this time a shadow, something, caused him to study the carved stone more carefully. Raging hot coals, the remnants of an earlier fire, glowed seductively in the hearth, their warmth dangerously friendly.

Jan stepped back looking at the mantle when suddenly he realized that the entire wall was a face, an enormous likeness of Lucifer! Horns curled up the wall to the vaulted ceiling. The fierce eyes bore down in accusation while the jaw and mouth opened into the fire pit. The only sound was that of his heartbeat. Here in stone was the medieval mind in all its fear and superstition.

"Jan?" Jacques called quietly.

Jan turned startled for a moment.

"Hello, Father. I've come to say goodbye and ask you to hear my confession."

The abbot looked into Jan's pleading eyes.

"Sit here. Tell me, what is troubling you?"

For the first time Jan laid out his life to a stranger; his mother's decision to ask him to leave her house, his aborted attempts at male prostitution, his meeting Tim and of his complicity as go between in an unholy bargain between his mother and Tim.

He revealed the events in Hungary and the secret society called Mundus. Lastly he spoke about his father's suicide. He accepted an enormous handkerchief from the priest, who spoke sincerely and compassionately.

"Those whom you, by rights, should be able to turn to have abandoned you. Why do you confess this to me? These are not *your* sins."

"I don't know!" Jan flung himself out of the chair, almost knocking it to the floor. He paced the room, trying to form words from his confusion.

"Right now all I can think about is Tim. The others seem as if they never existed. I think love him. What am I saying! I don't even know what I'm talking about! What do I know about love. Still, I'll do anything Tim asks. I've made a deal and I won't go back on it. But the sex! I mean I love the feeling of pleasing him and it feels good to me too. I won't deny that, but I still don't know if I'd go for it if my life was different."

Jan blew his nose into the cloth embossed with the abbey's crest. "Oh no! I just spread snot all over the cross!"

Jacques smiled. "It will wash out. Jesus was a human too. Do you not think his nose ran too when He wept?"

"I never thought about it that way."

"You know, Jan, we Catholics spend a lot of time worrying about how we should behave in our religion and not enough time living our faith. Religion and faith have very little in common. Faith is God's gift to us. Religion is how we express our thanks for that gift. Without exception we humans mess up the thank you card, no matter which God we adore."

Jan had never heard a priest talk this way. "How can you say this stuff? Won't you get into trouble?"

"Oh, I don't think so. After all, I am, as you Americans say, top dog around here."

"What should I do about the sex?"

"Sex and sexuality are wonderfully created by God. It is for us to express it to one another. How we do that should not be subject to fear or judgment from others and especially from ourselves. For us, as Catholics, it is very complicated, more than necessary, I believe. You see, the church entwines the pleasure of sex with its procreative objective. Then in the same breath we are told that the pleasure of sex is corrupt and so while we have sex, we should keep our eyes fixed on heaven. That's not only unrealistic but it is an uncomfortable position."

Jan blushed at the innuendo.

"And love? What about male to male love?" he asked.

"All I can tell you for certain that love is not a democratic emotion. If you are blessed and find love, then guard it. Never let yourself become indifferent to anyone you love or toward anyone who loves you. Above all, do not become careless with another human heart. Hearts are not nearly as resilient as skeptics and cynics like to pretend. Do you understand?"

"Yes, I know what you mean," Jan replied, "but doing it is not so easy."

"The first maxim of a physician is 'Do no harm.' It works well for loving one another too."

"Thank you, Father. For this, and for your friendship."

Jan knelt on the rough stone floor. As he received the absolution of the faithful, he prayed his contrition. "...and I detest all my sins, because I dread the loss of heaven and the pains of hell."

After embracing the monk in farewell, Jan walked back to the chateau.

CHAPTER 36

▼

Making his way back to the big house, Jan looked up at the slate colored sky. Great gray clouds masked the afternoon sun, forcing its rays to surrender their brilliance. Jan walked aimlessly through the narrow cobblestone lanes that lead out of town towards the chateau. A light mist, not yet a drizzle, matted his hair. The weather suited his mood. Arles usually hummed with the buzz of day to day living. Today it seemed the cloudbanks pressing down on the town had muted everything. He wondered if going deaf was like this, a faint awareness that sound was growing softer, like lost echoes.

The rutted road turned into a black mudslide, so Jan moved off across a fallow lavender field still firm ,with stubble. He remembered Tim's indulgent chuckle when he asked why the sky here was purple rather than blue.

"It's the sun's reflection on the lavender. They grow it here the way we grow wheat in Nebraska," Tim had said.

The turmoil of the past months moved around in Jan's mind like one of those hand-held plastic toys with the alphabet all mixed up. The challenge was to arrange all the letters in order from A to Z. He couldn't remember ever finishing one.

When he looked around, Jan found he had wandered into a zigzag maze of boxwood. It led to a disused fountain. The fine marble had been stripped away long ago, leaving only a ragged brick underlay. He sat on the fountain edge dangling his legs over the side. Below, the lichen-covered brickwork looked the way he felt, fragmented and not easily repaired.

"Can this really be happening to me? Do things like this happen to anyone? I'm young and I'm exhausted already! Nobody lives like this. That's just in movies. I do like the idea of money and power. I love Tim, at least as much as I can love anybody in just a few months. He's handsome, considerate and sexy. Sexy. Why do I think of him as sexy? Am I really gay? Mundus scares the shit out of me—"

Jan heard the crunch of gravel behind him. André, a thirty something gardener who had been at the chateau all summer, was a few feet away carrying a sickle in his right hand. Jan had seen him hanging around whenever he was exploring the grounds.

Jan looked up and squinted. "André? What do you want?"

"I want you! I have wanted you since I saw you," came his answer in clumsy English.

Jan looked at the man, then at the sickle and gave a short chuckle. "Well, you can't have me. I think you'd better go now before *Le seigneur* comes along."

André raised the sickle ever so slightly.

"Please, I don't want to hurt you…. Please!"

Jan knew he should be afraid. Sitting as he was with André towering over him, he was defenseless. André was heavier, stronger *and* armed. Still, Jan sensed that in reality he was the one in control. He was the master, André the servant.

He shook his head and smiled. Softly, he whispered, "You're not going to hurt me, André."

"How can you be so sure?"

"Because you want to make love to me, not hurt me. In the end you will do neither. Now go away. *Le seigneur* is coming behind you."

Tim waved and called out, "Jan, where have you been?"

Jan stood and brushed the damp soil from the seat of his pants.

"I've just been talking to André," he answered.

Tim joined them and stood beside the gardener.

"Tim," Jan said. "André wants to go to Lyon to try his hand at silk making. He asked me if I thought you would give him his wages now so that he can make his arrangements."

Tim looked at André, then back at Jan.

"When does he want to go?" Tim asked cautiously.

"Tonight," Jan said firmly.

André gave a sad shrug, turned to go and stopped for one last look at Jan's face.

Tim eyed André moving off across the smooth winter lawn.

"Do you think he'll be a good silk maker?" he asked,

"No," Jan said with barely concealed anger.

As they walked along Jan leaned over and pushed his head into Tim's shoulder.

"So, do you want to talk about it?" Tim asked.

"Not necessary…it's over now."

"Did you have a confrontation with André?"

"Something like that."

"How does it feel to leverage power for the first time?"

"Scary."

"Why, because it was so easy?"

Jan turned his face away.

"No, because I think I liked it."

Tim hugged him.

"You really are someone very special."

Jan hugged him back.

"So are you."

Later in the week they left for the drive north to Lyon and the airport. At the car, Jan stopped to take one last look at the estate. For the first time he noticed the de Main coat of arms above the main doors and the Latin motto over the ducal escutcheon. *Do Justice. Love Mercy. Walk Humbly in the Sight of Thy God.*

"That's really a beautiful expression," Jan said.

Tim was impressed.

"You really can read Latin!"

Jan smirked.

"Did you think I lied? Besides it's a simple style, not some obscure idiom or anything."

"Would you like to have it? The motto, I mean. I can have it transferred in your name if you'd like that as a Christmas present."

"Can you do that? Yeah! I'd like it a lot!"

"Peter was the last of his family. I own the estate, but not the title. It seems a shame that no one would ever use the motto. I think he would like you to have it."

Jan tearfully thanked him. He knew how much Tim loved the old man and how often he had gone off to visit Peter's mausoleum. Jan had gone there with him only once, feeling that it was rightfully a place for Tim alone.

CHAPTER 37

▼

The Christmas season passed in Philadelphia with a round of parties Tim had arranged to introduce Jan to his circle of friends. They spent New Year's Eve alone with music and a soft fire in the hearth.

He held Jan in a swaying embrace as they danced to Tony Bennett's "Because of You."

"You okay?" Tim asked.

"Sure. Why?"

"You're very quiet. Anything on your mind?"

"I'm fine. Just horny."

"Well then, let's go take care of business."

"Let's let the song finish," Jan said as they moved around in the half-light.

"You like Tony Bennett?"

"Tony who?"

"Lord!" Tim sighed.

The blissful days of the holidays passed too quickly for Jan. All of a sudden, it was time for work. And as always with Tim, there was no leading up to things. They happened just like that. Bam!

Preparing to go to the office after an urgent call from Marsha, Tim looked at Jan over the breakfast table.

"There's a brochure for Saint Joseph's College. It's in the office. I want you to look at it while I'm gone."

"You want me to look at a college?"

"Yes I do."

"You do?" Jan asked again.

Tim's face flushed, "What part of 'Yes I do' didn't you understand?"

Jan shifted uncomfortably in his seat.

Mrs. Santos walked Tim to the door. She caught his sleeve and said, "*Señor* Tim, don't be so hard on him. He is not responsible for what goes on in your office."

Tim nodded and left.

Staring at his coffee cup, Jan thought about what Tim had said. "If he thinks he's going to stick me back in school after what I went through this last summer, he's crazy!"

Mrs. Santos walked back into the kitchen and began loading the dishwasher. Jan went over to her.

"Mrs. Santos, what if I don't want to go to college?"

"*Señor* Jan, I have worked in this apartment for twenty-nine years and can tell you that what *Señor* Tim says is not an option. If he wishes it, you must comply. Do you understand? In every way you must obey him." Smiling, she tousled Jan's hair. "Trust me, you won't regret it."

In his office at the Templars of Law, Tim stood at his desk for a moment thinking about what Mrs. Santos had said to him as he left the apartment. He mashed down on the intercom button.

"Marsha," he said quietly, "I'm in my office."

Releasing the intercom control Tim slouched back in his high-backed leather chair and waited. Two minutes later Marsha was standing at West Point attention about to give the boss a client she sensed he wouldn't like.

Taking a deep breath she began, "The bishop of the Ship of Zion Rescue Ministry is scheduled to meet with us to talk about charges that he is responsible for the mass suicide of certain members in his congregation in Kentucky. He specifically asked for you."

"How did he get my name?"

"I'm not sure. He just had it."

"So what's the state's charge?"

"They say he's responsible for the suicide of an entire family, including their children, a total of six people. The state alleges that under the guise of Christian Fundamentalism, he indoctrinated them in a cult of fear. The note they left said something about being afraid of living among idolaters and going to hell." Marsha concluded, "I'm getting faxes from the Kentucky assistant DA's office as we speak."

Tim shook his head. "This doesn't make sense. His responsibility in a separate act is almost impossible to prove and the state can't prove malice unless he assisted in the acts. So what's he worried about?"

"He says he *is* guilty, that he was present when these poor people killed themselves and he wants to confess but doesn't want to get the death penalty. You have a reputation of getting the state to back off the needle."

"Kentucky is after the death penalty? What, they have an overstock of poison and are afraid it will go bad before it gets used? I'm not going down to Kentucky for this. Get—"

"He's here in Philly," Marsha said.

"Who's here?"

"The bishop, who have we been talking about?"

"What! And how did he get here? He didn't just get on a bus without the police knowing about it, did he?"

"Apparently he did," Marsha replied.

Tim mulled all this over in his head. It really was something a junior partner could handle. Finally, he said, "I'll talk to him, but I won't guarantee that I'll handle it myself. Call him and tell him the meeting is on for one o'clock."

"Actually he's here now. I tried to get him to go to a hotel but he said he didn't have the money for one. I offered the courtesy of our office funds, but he said no to that too."

"It's a good thing I came straight in then, isn't it? Tim let out a frustrated sigh, "Alright, I'll speak with him. But first I need to look up the criteria for a death penalty in Kentucky. Show our guest into the small conference room."

Marsha left Tim's office while he logged onto the Internet site listing details on the death penalty statutes for Kentucky. Satisfied, he walked the short hall that connected his office with the firm's conference rooms.

The accused bishop was standing with his back to the door looking out of the arched Palladian window when Tim entered the conference room. Walking across the small room, Tim extended his hand, then pulled back as if he had been bitten by a snake.

"How the hell did you get in here? Is this some kind of joke?" Tim roared.

It was Pastor Leo Robbins himself, the man responsible for driving Tim from his family and congregation. The frightening zealot, whose sermons left his teenage ears ringing, was now a man with bent shoulders. All the fire and brimstone seemed burned away.

"Marsha! Damn it, where are you?"

Marsha rushed in. "What's wrong? Are you alright?" she gasped.

The self-styled bishop had taken refuge behind a chair while Tim shook like a leaf in a hail storm.

"Marsha," Tim began, trying to control his temper. "I need to know the reason I was not given this man's name."

"I didn't think...I'm sorry." She made a helpless gesture. "He implied you knew each other. I'm sorry. I—"

"Leave us please. I'll speak with this man alone for a while. We'll be all right. I'll call you when we're through."

Tim stood trembling in a white rage. Summoning all the self-control he possessed, he turned to address the broken man and took a deep breath. All the denied hatred he had toward Robbins now welled up and demanded to be recognized.

"I'm told you want to confess your complicity in six deaths, but you're afraid to meet you maker just yet. I remember you saying that our whole lives were a rush into the Lord's arms. What happened? Did you trip or just get cold feet?"

Tim didn't wait for an answer. "I'll put the charge layman's terms for you so we understand each other. Kentucky alleges that you used texts from the Bible in order persuade two adults and four children into believing that if they continued to live they would be so corrupted in the eyes of God that they would lose their salvation and spend eternity in hell. As a direct result these innocent people took their own lives to in your words "escape damnation. It also states you were in the room when this occurred. In short these poor souls died because you told them to live would mean spiritual death. You hypocrite! You facilitated, albeit indirectly, in the deaths of people who trusted you. Do I have the basic facts correct so far?"

"Yes, but please, let me explain what happened," Robbins said weakly.

"You ignorant, bastard! I know exactly what happened! I was the recipient of your righteous words myself. I know what happens to earnest souls when they fall under the thrall of Bible pounding, hymn-singing sons of bitches like you! You knew what was best for me and you saw that I got it! Or have you forgotten?"

"You look as if you've done all right without God." Robbins observed dryly.

Tim leapt up and took Robbins by the throat. He stared into the man's bloodshot eyes and pushed him into a chair.

Tim began to speak very slowly and clearly, "I walked..., walked here to Philadelphia. Did you know it is exactly four hundred and sixty-seven miles and thirty-three feet from Little Fork to the Philadelphia city limits? Have you any idea how many times during that walk I turned around when I heard a car or truck, certain it would be you or my mom and dad come to carry me home. But it never happened! I walked every foot *alone!*" Tim shouted. "I was fourteen years old for god's sake, you rotten asshole!"

Tim closed his eyes and fought off the memory and then took a deep breath to calm down.

"For a year after I came to this city I watched for a familiar face. I thought, I'd be rescued soon. But Nobody came! Nobody came!" Tim yelled as he turned to keep from showing his tear filled eyes.

Robbins shook his head. "I failed you. I know."

Tim let a moment pass and wiped his eyes with a handkerchief.

"And now you're hoping *I* won't fail you. First you betray me and now you tempt me before Almighty God! You really know how to piss a guy off, don't you?"

Tim waked to the padded office door. Marsha was standing outside when Tim opened it.

"Please get the reverend on the first bus back to Frankfort." Then under his breath he said, "Get the phone number of the assistant DA working on the state's case."

Robbins was too busy worrying about his own skin to offer any information about Tim's kin back in West Virginia, and Tim didn't ask.

Back in his office, Tim saw the interoffice mail server flashing.

The message read, "The ADA for Kentucky vs. Robbins is Jason Mallory."

The phone number was listed. Tim and Jason Mallory had worked together as assistants for the New Jersey Supreme Court when they first passed the bar.

"This could be an advantage or a problem," Tim thought.

Jason had opted for the penury of a state job in Kentucky. Tim got rich. The two had been very competitive in school. Tim knew that Jason had kept tabs on his career. He dialed the number listed in the memo.

"Jason Mallory, please," Tim said.

"This is Mallory."

"Jason, it's Tim Morris. How are you, ole buddy?"

"Tim, wow! It's good to hear your voice! I'm fine. You know I got married to a local girl? No kids yet. How about you?"

"I hadn't heard you got married Congratulations! I'm fine. Nothing to report."

Tim had no intention of getting personal with a potential adversary.

After a pause, Jason said, "This isn't a social call, is it? We haven't exactly kept in touch."

"No. I'm sorry to say this is business. I have Leo Robbins as a client."

"I'm listening," Mallory said.

"Frankly I don't know what you've got that makes you think you can get a guilty verdict let alone a death sentence but it doesn't matter. He'll plead guilty to all charges. He'll take whatever you guys dish out if you'll drop the death penalty. At his age he'll die in prison anyway so the state gets to save on death row appeals."

"What if I can't deliver the plea?" Jason asked. "This was a very hot issue down here. This is the South Tim, not Boston or New York."

Tim gambled on his reputation. "Then he'll plead not guilty and I'll have to come down there and get him acquitted."

Jason paused and considered having to go up against the guy who beat him every time in mock trials.

"Give me an hour. I'll call back."

Tim was walking back to the Saint Roi when his cell phone rang.

"It's me," Marsha said, "Mallory called. They'll pick Robbins up when he gets off the bus. They're really cheesed that he left the state without them even noticing but you got your deal. The papers are being faxed. Do you want me to sign for you?"

"No. I'll sign *these* papers myself."

CHAPTER 38

▼

The chancellor of St. Joseph's College accepted the application from Jan's nervous hand, then ushered him out for a tour of the campus. Lyndon Hallowfield, a.k.a. Sir Lyndon Hallowfield, Knight Commander of the Most Excellent Order of the British Empire, was due to retire at the end of the school term. As chancellor, he had kept a watchful eye on Tim when he attended Saint Joe's. Peter de Main had asked it as a personal favor, and Lyndon was happy to oblige. Now Tim was asking for the same consideration of an old mentor.

"Tim, I'll recommend anyone you like if you feel the young man needs special attention. But I have to tell you, Jan's records from Saint Dominic's are very good on their own. Good enough academically that he doesn't need any supplemental recommendation. Where did you get the idea that he was a poor student?" Lyndon asked

"He said himself that he was a so-so student, and I took him at his word, although his grammar should have tipped me off that he was just being modest. Of course he speaks Philly lingo and teen slang, but when he's serious he's really quite eloquent."

Sir Hollowfield had been impressed during the interview. Not only were Jan's transcripts strong; his speaking ability, poise and confidence were exactly what "old world" Saint Joseph's strove to impart to its students.

Lyndon and Tim passed an hour sipping tea and reminiscing about Peter de Main. Lyndon was showing Tim a scale model of the new science wing when Jan returned to the office in the company of a sophomore pressed into acting as guide for mid-year applicants.

"Thank you, Paul, that will be all," said Lyndon.

The student guide left with a relieved smile.

Tim said, "Look you two I'm going for a walk around the quad. I'll be back in a few minutes."

Turning to Jan, Lyndon said, "Well Jan, how do you like our campus?"

"It's beautiful, like something you'd see in England."

"It does, doesn't it. Perhaps that's why I always felt comfortable working here."

"The new term begins the last week in January. Saint Joe's is honored to accept you into the college and I would personally like to welcome you, if it suites you.

"Oh. Yes very much," Jan said.

"Very well then."

Lyndon smiled and put his arm around Jan's shoulder.

"So you will have about a week to prepare. Here is a student guide book that details the orientation sessions you should attend."

"Thank you," Jan said, as he shook Hollowfield's hand mustering enthusiasm he didn't feel.

"Look, I'm going to wait in the car. OK?"

"Yes. Of course. I'll tell Tim where you are."

Lyndon and Tim walked down the brick and marble cloister that separated the general offices from the main campus. Old oaks haplessly threw their acorns across the manicured lawn in an attempt at procreation.

Finally Tim asked, "So how did it go? I mean, what do you think? Will he make out here?"

"Everything went very well. I offered him enrollment and he accepted. Don't worry too much about him. I think he'll be just fine here."

From inside the car, Jan watched the two men part with handshakes.

"Is Tim trying to ditch me? What's wrong with me? Why does everybody leave me?" he asked himself. He had thought about this ever since Tim had mentioned college. First his dad, then Father Sobinski, then, his mother and now Tim.

Tim plopped into the driver's seat and shivered. "Damn it's cold in here! Why didn't you turn the heater on?"

"Self-abasement. I'm giving way to saintly neurosis," Jan joked.

"Let me know if you plan to do it often this winter, I may need to buy some earmuffs! Seriously though, Lyndon said he thinks you'll do just fine here. You don't seem too happy being accepted. What's wrong?"

"It's not the school," Jan said. "I used to dream about going to a good school instead of being stuck in vocational classes learning how to paint battleships. But I have to tell you, I'm tired. Sobinski's pushed me all last summer so I could get my diploma before he left for Rome. And then my mother asked me to leave. We go to Europe and some lady gets her throat cut right in front of me. We just got back home and now college? I feel like I'm in a play where I have to act out all the parts all at the same time. You've worn me out. I just want to live with you. Can't we just do that?"

"Jan do you know how bored you would get in a year of doing nothing but lazing around? In no time you would be drinking and eventually you would be drinking too much and after that it would be hello Betty Ford. Do you have any idea how widespread alcohol abuse in the gay community is, not to mention downright alcoholism? Spending life in a drunken stupor is not what I wanted for myself, and I'm not going to enable you to find it either."

"That's not what I'm talking about. I just want to be with you."

"Every one of us looks for the quickest way to his heart's desire. But look, I'm a full adult with responsibilities to others as well as you and myself. You on the other hand are just beginning to see the world, my world. It's the one you'll live in with me, but it's a complicated place to be in so you have to be ready for it. There's just no getting around it."

Jan sat nodding. "Okay, you win. I'll give it my best shot. Just don't expect me to be happy about it."

Tim whistled all the way back to the city. "God I'm good!"

During his first few months at Saint Joe's, Jan would slam his books into a backpack and race back to the Saint Roi and to Tim; each time he worried he would be turned away at the entrance by the doorman Eventually, though, he calmed down and even stayed on Fridays at the school for lectures and an occasional show at the college theater. It took a while but he began to realize that Tim was really going to be there, waiting for him always. As the end of the spring term drew near, Tim took him aside.

"Jan, you have a decision to make."

Jan thought, "This is it...Tim's finally decided to ditch me."

"Ugh! Another one? What now?"

"I have to be in Taipei in mid-summer. You can stay for summer classes, or come with me."

"There are some classes I'd like to take, but I want to be with you too."

"There'll be time for you to think about it. Pat Hunter has built a house near the shore and invited us for a couple of weeks. We'll get some leisure time together. And there'll be a lot of men down there, very wealthy men."

"So? I don't need to be around other men. I love *you*," Jan said

CHAPTER 39

▼

Han and Joy strolled hand-in-hand along South Street. The aroma of roasting souvlakia mixed with Cajun catfish and Philly cheese steaks drew noisy crowds out onto the narrow sidewalks.

"Hungry?" Joy asked.

"For you," Han replied.

"I mean for food, silly."

"I can take a hint. What are you in the mood for?"

"How about we go to the Warsaw Café?"

"Sounds good to me. Want to taxi or walk?"

"Walk, of course. I need the exercise."

Han noticed Joy was nervously looking around the whole time they were walking.

"What are you looking for, another bargain?" he asked.

"No, I'm always afraid I'll run into Jan. Well, not afraid, I just…, nothing."

Han was about to say something when suddenly a car came out of nowhere. By the time he realized what was happening a sedan had smashed across a line of parking meters, picking Joy up in the grill and carrying her through the glass window of Forever Memories Bridal shop.

Instinctively, Han dropped to his knees. Noises poured in and out of his head like a badly tuned carousel. Someone stepped on his hand in a mad rush for safety. People ran screaming while mounted police reined in their horses. Sliding over glittering glass the big animals snorted wet exhaust into the chilly spring air. A curious crowd drawn by the commotion, formed on the other side of narrow street.

Joy's smashed body lay as if she had been caught napping. The only evidence that she was dead was a line of red drool weeping from the corner of her mouth. Like an unsure lover, Han tenderly lifted her in his arms.

A cop tapped his shoulder. "Hey buddy, do you know this woman?"

"Yeah," he answered numbly.

Han looked around. His ears were ringing and his head hurt.

"What?...What, happened?"

"Uh, Some guy jumped the curb," the cop said.

Han flashed his Interpol identification. "Mind if I take a look?"

The cop's eyes popped. "Be my guest."

Han kissed Joy's cooling forehead and laid her ever so gently on the display window floor. He pulled the train from a fallen mannequin and covered her with the white satin. He stood forcing his professional persona to take charge of the private man.

"Get a curtain over the window, will you? She shouldn't be lying out where people can see her," Han said.

"Sure, I'll do that right now."

Han went around to the driver's side of the car and looked in. The windshield bore a shattered oval where the man's head had smashed the tempered glass. The man was dead.

"He should have worn his seat belt," Han said dryly. "Any I.D. on him?"

A cop fished through the dead man's pockets, retrieving a wallet and a Serbian passport.

Han read the name. Stanos Moldine.

"Fuck!" Han shouted.

"Mister, if you know anything about this man we need to know," the cop said.

"What I know is the guy is dead. If I learn more I'll let you know," Han answered.

Still somewhat dazed, Han walked around to Joy's body. A late-arriving police woman tried to push him back.

"I was with the lady. I'm going to sit with her until she's moved." Han's grim face beat back any objections the officer may have had.

Later that evening Tim was dozing while a motet by Ippolitov Ivanov soothed away a hard day at the office. The phone seemed so out of place with the soft strains of the Russian Hymn *O Gentle Light of the Holy Glory*.

"This is Tim," he answered sleepily.

"Tim, we need to meet right now," Han said.

"You sound upset. Come on over."

"No. Meet me at the Venture. Something's happened, and I don't' want to be spotted at the Saint Roi."

When Tim walked into the Venture Inn, he saw Han sitting red-eyed at the far end of the bar. The only other customer was a man blubbering into his beer something about the inconstancy of love. Johnny Mathis moaned, "What I Did for Love" from the jukebox. Pat Hunter was talking with Han as Tim slid onto a low barstool.

"What's going on?" Tim asked.

"Joy Phillips is dead. A car tried to run us down. I think I was the intended target."

Tim tried to process the words, but his brain refused to work Before he could ask, Han replayed the events of the past three hours in a monotone matching his despair. He ended with the driver's name.

"Moldine!" Tim caught himself, remembering he was in a public place.

Just then, Han's cell phone rang. "Han here." He listened to the caller's report. "Thanks. I'll pass it along."

"That was Interpol. Remember the woman who tried to kill you in Budapest? The driver who drove the car was her brother."

"Why didn't Interpol have this guy in their sites?" Tim demanded angrily.

"Why didn't the FBI figure out 9/11 in advance? Stuff gets through," Han said.

"I've got to tell Jan. I don't know what to say. I don't know how he'll react."

"I'd like to be there, if it's okay with you."

"Sure, but don't tell him about you and Joy. I don't want him linking this with Mundus."

"But it *is* linked—"

Tim held up a hand. "Budapest was an aberration, and I don't want Jan to get the idea that a lunatic fringe is after us."

"What you're trying to do is protect him from a nasty side of life and keep yourself out of hot water," Han accused.

"It's my decision," Tim said.

"You're the boss. Just remember I told you so."

"Meet us tomorrow at the Adelphia Tavern at around two."

He gave Han a weak smile of gratitude and left.

Tim got home around midnight. Jan was sitting in the dark.

"Where have you been?" he asked.

"I was talking to Han—" Tim stopped short. Jan had been crying.

"There was a news item on TV. I heard my mom's name. I saw Han. What's going on?"

"Han was with her when it happened. Some guy jumped the curb."

"That can't be all there is to it. What was he doing with her anyway?"

"They had been seeing each other since he got back from Budapest. It looks like Han was a target for assassination."

Jan jumped up. "Hold it!" he shouted. "You mean they've been together *all* this time and you never said a word to me about it! She'd be alive if he had left her alone. Do *you* think it was okay for him to be with her?

"He asked what I thought and I said I couldn't see why not."

"You couldn't see why not! The man is a thug! He hurts people for a living! This was my mother for God's sake...not some dockside harlot!"

"May I remind you that it was your *mother* who brought you to me and walked away with the money."

"Don't you even go there, Tim!"

Jan collapsed onto the sofa and grabbed a pillow to his chest. Shaking his head in bewilderment, he looked at Tim with new eyes.

"How could you do this to me? What have ever I done to you? I obeyed you in everything. Nothing was too hard, because I loved you so much. I thought you felt proud of me and that made me feel proud of myself. For once in my life I was confident in our life together."

"Jan that's not fair! You're angry and it's normal to lash out, but neither your mother nor Han is responsible for this. And if it's any consolation, the driver is dead."

"Consolation! Are you crazy? Ever since I met you all I've done is cry and worry that you're going to get me killed. I...I..., oh hell!"

Jan headed for the door. "I've got to tell my family"

Tim stopped him.

"Your sisters and brother are okay. Your Aunt Susan has them at her house."

Jan broke down in Tim's arms. They walked to the bedroom.

"You need to rest. There are decisions you need to make with a clear head. But they can wait until tomorrow."

CHAPTER 40

▼

Anger and continuing doubts about his relationship with Tim stole Jan's sleep until the wee hours. He wanted to blame Tim for his mother's death. She didn't know any dangerous people—except Han. Han and his mother? Jan didn't want to think about them together. What would happen to his sisters and brother? He hadn't slept long. It was eight o'clock when Mrs. Santos knocked on the bedroom door before entering with a cup of coffee. Jan never grew out of liking it the way she had first mixed it for him when came to live at the Saint Roi. He reached out and hugged her tightly.

"I am so sorry, little one. I will pray for you and your poor mama," she said.

"Thanks. You have been like a second mother to me. I love you, Mrs. Santos."

"And I love you as well. *Señor* Tim is in the office. He wants to see you when you're ready to talk."

Jan nodded. "I'll be there after I shower."

Twenty minutes later, he flopped into the oversized chair by the desk. He didn't like Tim very much at the moment, and it showed. He was back to feeling that Tim was in some way responsible for his mother's death.

Tim studied Jan carefully. He pulled out a sheaf of papers. "You've got some decisions to make about this situation. I can help you with the details but—"

"Hold it. Details? Decisions? More Mundus crap? What do *I* have to do with it?"

"Not Mundus, family," Tim said patiently. "You are the oldest adult son, and in the absence of a will the law recognizes you as the executor of your mother's estate. As far as we can tell, she left no will. That's not unusual. Most people don't think of wills until they're ill or old. No one expects to die young."

Jan sat in sullen silence. He really didn't care about wills. How could Tim be so cold?

"What do I have to do?" he asked sourly.

Tim was tired. He'd been on the phone with Jan's Aunt Susan. She didn't like the interference and even suggested a lawyer of her own. Tim patiently explained that he was acting as Jan's attorney and she had no choice but to let Jan have a free hand in settling his mother's estate. They agreed that Joy's house was to be sold and the proceeds turned over to Susan as a gift.

He explained these details for Jan's approval, adding. "Han has set up trust funds for your sisters and your brother. Their education will be paid for up to and including graduate work with a cash payout at age twenty-five of one million dollars each. All I need is your signature authorizing Templars to manage the estate. The funeral will be the day after tomorrow. Han made the arrangements. He paid for it too."

Jan wanted to argue against the merits of Han's generosity, but he couldn't think of any credible reasons. Had he done this to purge his feelings of guilt or was there more? At any rate his sisters and brother couldn't have dreamed of getting such a sum of money in their wildest imagination. Even if they weren't financial successes in life they would still be taken care of. He simply picked up the pen, signed the authorization papers and said coldly, "I've got to get back to school."

*   *   *   *

The next two days passed in slow motion for Jan. Dealing with the funeral seemed surreal.

"This can't be happening to me," he told himself repeatedly.

Finally, he found himself alone with his mother's coffin, engaging in a one-sided dialogue of sorrow and regret. At his request, the box was sealed. The idea of people staring at his dead mother made him sick. He remembered the circus of family and friends that convened at his father's funeral and was determined it would not be repeated.

Father Orloff offered the Requiem Mass, and Joy's daughters read the prayers for the dead. Han, along with Jan's Uncle Bob, were among the pallbearers. Jan went through the motions, shaking hands with people he had never met or no longer remembered, drying tears that seemed to never stop flowing.

Tim drove him back to the Saint Roi after the burial. That night their love-making was furious, both intent on exorcising devils through a passion neither of them understood.

As the months went on, Jan lost himself in study, parties and amateur theater. Thoughts of his mother, the funeral and all that had happened muddled in the haze of time. Opera galas in foreign capitals with Tim were especially heady times, even for a man growing in sophistication. He was maturing, growing, in charm and appeal. Invitations from men and women with addresses on the Rue San Honoré and Park Avenue filled his little black book. Notes were passed to Jan surreptitiously in handshakes but he never replied. It became a game where hope played the tease and Jan enjoyed it. Tim was looking older and Jan assumed it was the strain of Mundus wearing on him. Worldwide terrorism made his presence evermore urgent in places like Nepal, Israel, and the Philippines.

Jan spent part of his summers alone in Arles managing the chateau that one day would be his. European heads of Mundus often stayed there briefing him on the societies overall successes and failures. But Jan's involvement with Mundus was still limited.

At home, Mrs. Santos was slowing from her usual energetic pace; teatime was becoming naptime. Her daughter Sonya helped at the Saint Roi. Tim had asked Sonya if she would become a permanent fixture at the apartment.

"Yes," she said. "I'd like that very much."

CHAPTER 41

▼

Winter rain tore at the city. Wind smacked the heavy glass windows, making them shake.

A fire at his back, Jan sat in the study reading one of Tim's journals about another man who had lived in the thirteenth floor apartment of the Saint Roi. Jan wasn't sure what he was searching for or even what he would find in the journals. All residents of the apartment had been masters of Mundus, each chosen by a previous occupant of this most remarkable space. Jan was certain there was a mystical connection between Mundus and the Saint Roi, though he had found nothing yet to support his hunch.

Tim had begun writing at age twenty-five, soon after that Peter died. Tim was now forty. The fifteen volumes in Tim's hand were in a special place along the wall.

Jan's eyes wandered from the hand written pages to the windows. The wet skyscrapers looked like giant fingers poking insolently into God's face. He wondered if nature was trying to punish the city. Earlier in the year the city released several mating pairs of peregrine falcons to help in controlling an exploding pigeon population. Tim had encouraged a pair to set up house on the window ledge. The two birds looked cold and wet. If the rain didn't break soon they would spend the night hungry.

Mrs. Santos broke into his thoughts, knocking at the study door. "I've got a tray of tea sandwiches and coffee for you," she announced.

"Mrs. Santos! What a nice surprise," Jan said as he slipped the journal into the desk drawer.

Smiling, she shook her head. "You do not have to hide the journal from me, *Señor* Jan. I read them all many years ago."

"You've read the journals? All of them?" Jan said, incredulous.

"Oh yes. My husband and I were members of Mundus in Chile. When Pinochet came to power he was arrested and executed in a soccer stadium with many others. No one will ever know how many. I came here to work for Mundus and *Señor* Peter."

"But if you're a Mundus member why do you do housework?"

"Because I need a job. We all can not all be big shots in the world," she laughed. "It is also a good cover for me when I must get deeply involved in an operation. But, I must tell you that I have been very inactive in Mundus since *Señor* Peter died. I am happy to serve as an advisor now."

Jan knew his next remarks might be impertinent, but he went ahead.

"Mrs. Santos, Tim told me about his childhood in West Virginia and how happy he was as a little boy. And he told me about the minister who was responsible for his being driven out of his home and church. Is there more?"

He bit into a sandwich waiting for Mrs. Santos to object to the direction the conversation was taking. She didn't.

"I was wondering," he continued. "When did he meet Peter? Did he live in the city with someone before they met?"

When Mrs. Santos didn't answer Jan gulped some coffee and said, "Umm…, When we're together…,Umm in bed…, God this is tough." He blushed.

She smiled. "*Señor* Jan, I am a woman of the world. You cannot shock me with bedroom tales. Please, ask your question."

"Did something happen to Tim? When we are together in bed our lovemaking is well, strange. It's like he's angry. He's never hurt me—well, not really—nor said anything to me, so I don't think he's angry with me so there has to be something eating at him. When he saw that Mrs. Santos was not uncomfortable, he continued, "Once he called me Wil. When I asked him who Wil was he got real upset. Who was he? Do you know?"

"Mrs. Santos drew a deep breath and nodded. "*Si,* I can tell you. The first year he was in the city *Señor* Tim suffered terrible indignities. He is a good man and a dreamer, but when he first came circumstances stole from him the wonder and excitement of a first love—of a first kiss with a loved one. He did not experience the sweetness of the sexuality he found. That is a special thing no matter who you are. He met this Wil person when he first came to Philadelphia. He used *Señor* Tim as a prostitute. But *Señor* Tim was smart even when he was so young. For a year, he collected enough money to run away. It was then he met *Señor* Peter.

After *Señor* Peter died, *Señor* Tim grew lonely. He began to bring street boys here. He told me he hoped one day he could save someone from the life he had. But I think he also wanted his lost innocence returned to him through whoever he helped. But he cannot find this because once it is taken it is gone forever. It is this knowledge that *Señor* Tim fights because deep in his heart he knows he cannot have it back and this frustrates him. Do you understand?"

Jan nodded solemnly. "Yes, I think so."

Mrs. Santos said, "It is like Indian warriors who ate the hearts of their enemies to gain their courage, *Señor* Tim has tried to take back his childhood from you by loving you."

She told Jan the story of Tim's first year in Philadelphia and the day she first met him. "Oh, he was a very angry boy. He was dirty and so was his dog."

"I always meant to ask about the picture of Tim and the Scottie dog. He looks so happy." Jan said.

"That picture was taken a year after he came here. The first few months were very bad. He yelled and was angry always. *Señor* Peter was so patient and kind to him. It was the kindness that he finally felt and accepted. When the little dog died, *Señor* Tim made his bed so wet with tears that the pattern on the mattress faded away. After that, until you came he would permit no pets or growing plants, nothing he could love or care for in the apartment. He even said to me once that he did not want to be responsible for another living thing ever again. Of course he is much changed now and after he found you. It is like when *Señor* Peter was alive."

Jan nodded. "Because he saved a boy whore he's purged of guilt."

"What a thing to say! Fate brought you together in a flower shop. You were gathered from a garden, not scraped from a gutter. That is how he saw it and so should you."

Jan stood and wrapped his arms around her. "Mrs. Santos, you overwhelm me."

CHAPTER 42

▼

Tim had had a busy week and made the best of this Saturday afternoon by easing his mind with lazy rest. A dinner party for that evening in Jan's honor was all set and ready to go. Tim's nine best friends had accepted the invitation to attend.

Jan had graduated the previous week from Saint Joseph's College earning two degrees, one in international law and the other in microbiology. He called it hedging his bets. Certainly, Tim's protégé had come a long way from the angry young man who resisted the idea of college and change. Now moved out and living in an apartment near the college, Jan was bringing a guest himself tonight, a woman he'd met in one of his classes.

Tim picked up his keys and headed for the door when the phone reserved for special calls rang. His heart gave a jump as it always did when he heard Jan's voice.

"Hi! I was wondering if I could stay over tonight," Jan said.

"Of course. What a question," Tim answered.

"Well, I didn't know if you were staying in the city or going to the shore for one last weekend before the season ends."

"No, I've closed everything for the winter. We've got a new client and I'll be handling the account until it gets established. One of the juniors can pick it up after I get the kinks worked out, but it'll be time consuming. You'll be here around seven, right?"

"Correct. See you then," Jan answered.

Tim wandered over to the window. Picking up his binoculars, he trained them on the bus stop. The covered kiosk, in reality just a battered box, was big enough for three or four people. It looked the same as it did the day Jan got off the # 27 bus from Kensington. Scenes from that day leapt from Tim's memory like clowns from a circus car.

Suddenly, he was brought out of his daydreaming by a key turning in the door lock. Mrs. Santos had arrived to begin preparing the dinner. Her menu was, as always, a guarded secret for these kinds of occasions and the cuisine was sure to be *non-parile*.

Making a beeline for the kitchen, she called out, "*Señor* Tim, do you want me to serve buffet style or restaurant style tonight?"

Tim considered a moment. "Mrs. S, make it easy on yourself. Whatever you decide will be fine."

"Easy on myself!" Mrs. Santos laughed. "If it were any easier here I'd be retired."

Jan arrived at seven on the dot. Tim, who hated it when anyone kept him waiting, had taught him punctuality and taught it well. He entered the apartment as quietly as he could and peeked into the kitchen, where Mrs. Santos was ladling fruit sauce over an exotic game bird.

"Um! Mrs. Santos what have we here?" Jan teased as he scooped a dollop of whipped cream into his mouth.

"*Ai, muchacho*! How many times have I told you? No little ones in my kitchen until I am ready," she admonished. "*Sin vergüenza*! You shameless one!"

Jan beamed his melt-your-heart smile, and the housekeeper's stern frown vanished. "Mrs. Santos, what would I do without you?"

"You'd get skinny like when you first came here."

Jan's smile faded as he slowly walked to the master bedroom. "*When you first came here.*" As he turned the words over in his mind, Tim dashed in with the grandest bouquet of calla lilies Mrs. Santos had ever seen. Hurrying past the kitchen door he said, "Please put these in some water, Mrs. S. I lost track of the time."

Jan was putting studs in a new formal shirt when Tim walked up. Giving Jan a hug, he said, "I'll just get a quick shower and be right with you. Make sure everyone gets settled, okay?"

At seven fifty-five the phone rang. "Your guests are on their way up," the lobby attendant said. At eight sharp Jan opened the door for Tim's closest friends, all looking like tipsy penguins out for a stroll. These nine men had been friends for many years, enduring, despite their personal differences. Jan looked each one over as they entered.

Jon Martin and Bill Cold were lawyers, Steve Slank and Barry Ross architects and part owners of the Penn Central Towers, Erik Wy a research scientist at a pharmaceutical firm and his longtime partner Jason Gill chief executive of an oil company. As always, Pat Hunter was a welcome guest. Rounding out the list were Carlo d'Maio and Jim Taylor. Carlo owned the five-star restaurant La Favorita. Jim was Carlo's bodyguard. Jan wondered why Carlo needed a guard but thought it best not to know.

Over these few past years, each of them, in his own way, had had a hand in polishing Jan from a beautiful, androgynous boy into a shining, handsome man. Jan felt he owed them much, but they would have denied it.

These men were not only Tim's friends; they had been his mentors as well. Jan wondered what the attraction might be. Money, certainly; power, absolutely; sex, unlikely. Over the years Tim had shared portions of his life's story with him, but Jan knew that much went unsaid.

Jan greeted each man by name. He started to close the door when Angela Alford arrived. She was dressed in a long sleeveless gown of black crepe d'chine. A single strand of pearls and hint of lipstick made her look fresh and classy.

"I hope I'm not late," she said.

"No. Not at all," Jan answered. After she settled in, Jan walked her to the bar, a mahogany Raffles-style table spread with fine spirits. The men had already gathered there. Angela asked for red wine.

"Hmm, no wine," he said apologetically. "I'll ask Mrs. Santos to get a glass for you."

He turned just as Mrs. Santos appeared, as if by magic, bearing a glass of Tyrone crystal three-quarters filled with a '74 Côte d' Rhone.

"How did she know?" Angela asked.

"That woman can hear a mouse tip-toe on cotton," Jan said.

Mrs. Santos turned away toward the kitchen, trying to remember what Han Ward used to say about trouble and women.

Jon Martin led the pack as each man sauntered over to them. Jan made the introductions, whispering into Angela's ear, "Don't try to remember their names; in an hour they won't be able to remember yours."

"Cynicism?" she said. "That's not like you."

"Congratulations, my boy," Jon hailed as he pumped Jan's hand. "What are your plans now, more school or a try at money making?"

"I'm off to the École Polytechnique for a year. Then I'll be back states-side. I hope to do some gene research consultation with DuPont. You know, saving the environment by making plastic out of air and dirt."

Jon was about to comment further when Tim joined the group. Sliding one arm around Angela's waist and hugging Jan's shoulders with the other, he announced that dinner was served.

Angela offered her hand to Tim. "It's a privilege to be here, Mr. Morris."

"Please call me Tim. And I'd he honored if you'd sit by me tonight."

Angela flushed modestly. "Yes of course," she said.

The conversation around the twelve foot long banquet table centered on the spiraling economy, corporate responsibilities to employees and Mrs. Santos' marvelous cuisine. Tim was happy to hear Jan and Angela join in the lively banter.

Tim's custom was to serve a glass of water to his guests as a signal that the party had ended, thus avoiding offense to anyone who might be tempted to overstay his welcome. Mrs. Santos entered at midnight with a tray with twelve glasses, which she placed to the right of each plate. Jan had warned Angela about this custom and so she rose with the men as they prepared to leave.

Tim and Jan walked everyone to the door expressing thanks and best wishes all around. Angela linked arms with two of the men as they wobbled down the hall toward the elevators.

"Whew," Jan exclaimed as he shut the bedroom door. "What a night! Tim, can you get everyone's address for me? I've got envelopes from each of them and I've a pretty fair idea what's in them. I'll need to send thank you notes."

"No problem. I'm bushed," Tim replied stripping off the last of his tuxedo.

Jan was already naked. He sat on the edge of the bed.

"I wish my mom could have been at the graduation," he said. "I think she would have been proud to be there."

"Yes, I'm sure she would," Tim answered softly.

They slid under the cool sheets and embraced. Tim fell on Jan as if he wanted to devour him. Jan submitted to Tim's passion until he too had heated to the boiling point. Jan worked with his mouth and hands until Tim fell back emptied and sated, out of breath and smiling like a Cheshire cat.

"Who taught you how to do that?" Tim asked.

"A master," replied Jan.

They drifted off in the untroubled sleep of a dead pope.

*   *   *   *

The sound of rings being pulled across a drapery rod woke Tim. Jan was standing before one of the full-length bedroom window. The bright morning light outlined Jan's naked body, making it glow against the pale fabric that guarded their privacy.

"Can't sleep?" Tim asked.

Jan didn't turn around. "I've met a girl."

Tim let a few moments pass, and then in a low voice said, "I met her last night, didn't I?"

"Yes."

"Is this serious?"

"As serious as it gets, I guess."

"How long have you known her?'

Jan shrugged. "About nine months."

Tim could only imagine what Jan must have been going through. Establishing a relationship is difficult enough straight or gay. By all rights, having two of them at the same time should have made Jan a basket case.

"Do want to marry her?" he asked.

"I want to but can't see how. You of all people should understand."

"Jan, you've always been free to go. I destroyed your mother's contract the day after she signed it."

"What do you mean? Are you saying I could have walked out of here all along?"

Tim could see Jan's cheeks flush with anger. He held up a hand in warning.

"Jan, don't say anything you'll regret later."

"You bastard! You sucked and fucked me silly, had me every way from Sunday. You pushed me until I was ready to drop! I've been groomed like a racehorse that doesn't want to race. Now you calmly sit there as if I should just take this in stride. Don't say anything I'll regret? What the *hell* do you know about regret?"

Tim answered in as patient a voice as he could muster. "How many times did you want to leave either out of self-doubt or remorse? How often were you discouraged enough to abandon school? How many times did your sense of responsibility to yourself keep you from sliding back to Kensington? How many times did you lie beside me after making love, hating me, hating yourself, your mother, everyone? All this has brought you to where you stand today. You're young, handsome, educated, soon to be employed and best of all you're in love. Just what the *hell* are you complaining about?"

"I was bought and paid for remember?" Jan cried. "Just like one of your expensive knickknacks, I was an ornament for your pride. You have no idea how many people tried to handle me. Some tried to buy me away from you. Did you know that?"

Tim shuddered a sigh. "No. I didn't..., I'm sorry"

"You didn't? Well, Tim, I guess I shouldn't be too surprised. You were so busy being proud of your creation you ignored fingerprints strangers left all over your precious possession."

"Jan, the contract was between your mother and me. Nowhere did it detail any responsibilities on your part. You want me to remember I bought and paid for you? Well Mister, I want you to remember that it was *you* who wanted this arrangement. You sought it out. It was you who came here to sell your ass. I didn't go to Kensington looking for poor Jan Phillips, or have you forgotten?"

Tim shook with rage and anguish. He paused a while then looked Jan in the face.

"You must have realized that you were of age and could leave anytime. I couldn't have stopped you.... As far as I'm concerned you got what you came for, money, comfort, and *power*."

Jan slumped onto the bed. The room was cool but he was flushed with exhaustion. Tim just didn't understand. The smartest, most sensitive man he ever knew didn't get it! Maybe it was his fault. Maybe he hadn't explained or asked or demanded or complained enough to make himself heard. Yet, Jan reasoned, Tim had got his money's worth. He forced the gall building in his throat back down.

He shook his head and looked sideways at Tim and said, "I guess I didn't think about it. I was happy. Like you said love makes us careless, especially with ourselves. I just couldn't fight the fantasy you had of me, the image I let you create, because you needed it so much. Comfort? Money? Power? Yeah, I got it all! But what you never realized was all I *ever* needed was to be wanted....not as a trophy or a cloned successor to your ambitions in Mundus or even as a memory of what you and Peter were—but, needed for *me*. Angela wants *me*. She doesn't know about the money or the power and she certainly has never heard of Mundus. All she sees is me. She loves me and it hasn't cost a cent. Can *you* beat that?"

A long pause hung between them Tim didn't want any more words to kill what had already been grievously injured.

"You'd better get your shower now. You and Angela have a date, don't you?"

"How did you know that?' Jan asked.

Tim just looked away.

A few minutes later Tim could hear the unmistakable sounds of crying. In the early days, whenever Jan was sad, he would sit under the shower spray and cry until he had no more tears or until all the hot water was gone. Usually his tears outlasted the water. It had been a long time since Tim had heard that sound. He felt like crying too but was afraid to give substance to fear.

Jan left later in the day without saying goodbye. He and Mrs. Santos walked to the street, where they parted company. She boarded the bus to her home in Upper Darby while Jan slipped into a waiting cab that would get him back to the Saint Joe's campus just in time to make his date with Angela.

Tim watched them from the window, then quietly closed the drapes.

✳   ✳   ✳   ✳

Two weeks later Tim heard from Jan. His voice mail was brief.

"I'm safe and sound in Lyon. Everyone has been great so far but I miss home already and can't wait to get back," adding, "Say hello to everybody for me."

Jan returned home twelve months later; home to Kensington, to his Aunt Susan's house not the Saint Roi and Tim.

The bans of marriage for Angela and Jan were read from Saint Dominic's Church pulpit shortly after his homecoming. Tim saw him only once more before the wedding. The encounter was accidental and brief. Jan was entertaining Angela and her parents at the Adelphia Tavern when Tim arrived with a sultan of some miniature emirate.

Jan watched hollow stomached as the robed potentate and Tim slipped into the cozy confines of one of the private nooks the Adelphia reserved for special guests. Tim looked back and gave a hopeful smile before sliding the pocket door closed. Jan looked back to Angela as she finished telling a joke. Everyone at the table laughed. All through the meal, Jan stole furtive looks at the enclosure where Tim and his guest sat fixing some knotty problem or other. He wondered if Tim was as jarred by his presence as he was of Tim's. Jan delayed their departure as long as he reasonably could but Angela's mother complained she was tired and wanted to leave.

After dropping her parents off at the hotel, he and Angela walked hand in hand to the Astral Plane restaurant for a nightcap.

"What's wrong?" Angela asked.

"Nothing. What makes you say that?"

"Well, for starters, Tim didn't come over to the table to say hello and you spent a lot of time sneaking peeks at the banquette."

"I was hoping to speak to him but I guess he was too busy to break away. By the way, did you see that guy's robes? They reminded me of that Carol Burnett skit where she wears a dress made from drapes and she leaves the curtain rod in it! That was so funny!"

"You're changing the subject."

When Jan didn't reply, Angela asked, "Excited about the wedding?"

"Terrified. How about you?"

"Terrified. Yeah, that about says it all."

"Is your mom okay with having the wedding at Saint Dom's? I know it's supposed to be in the bride's parish church, but Sobinski said he couldn't get the time to fly all the way to the West Coast. As it is he'll have to leave right after the Mass."

"Oh, no, she's fine with it," Angela lied.

The truth was her mother hit the roof when Angela explained the situation. Maxine Alford had ruled her family in ways a psychologist would have termed sociopathic. Her need to control every aspect of her surroundings made just being around her a toxic experience. She only relented when her husband, Douglas, pointed out that Angela was not a particular good catch and he'd be willing to have the wedding in hell to be rid of the girl.

CHAPTER 43

▼

The wedding at Saint Dominic's Basilica was the usual Catholic affair. La Favorita catered the meal courtesy of Carlo d' Maio. The bride's parents looked decidedly uncomfortable. They probably had never seen a place like Kensington before and earnestly wished the experience had been put off. Father Sobinski, now a monsignor, flew in especially for the occasion. He offered the Nuptial Mass along with two of Jan's priest teachers.

Jan's twin sisters, both with husbands of their own in tow, were attendants. His adopted brother and baby sister thought the whole thing was a little over the top.

Mrs. Santos sniffled her happiness mixed with foreboding into a handkerchief.

Han scared the shit out everybody in the congregation except for those who had met him earlier.

Tim sat with a smile of reassurance painted on his face just incase Jan looked his way. He didn't.

After the reception in Saint Dominic's parish hall, the happy couple left for a honeymoon in Italy.

The sun was low in the sky when Tim got home from the wedding. At this time of day, the surrounding big buildings skewed the light, often casting a sullen mood in the apartment. A courier had left a large envelope with the reception desk. It was from a photographer in Manhattan. Tim closed the penthouse door behind him and picked up a letter opener he kept on nearby stand. Slipping the sharp blade across the top flap, he extracted a black and white picture of Jan. The photographer apologized profusely explaining that the September Eleventh attack in New York had delayed shipment. Apparently, the envelope had languished in a New Jersey Post office for months before it was found in an unsorted batch of mail and returned to the photographer. Tim had bought a silver frame for the photo the year before and had forgotten all about it. He found it inside the bedside table. Slipping the picture into the frame, he put it on the bureau where he could see it easily from the bed.

Returning to the living room, Tim retrieved a cut crystal glass from the Raffles bar, poured himself a Scotch over ice then slumped into his favorite club chair by the window. As a rule he didn't suffer from headaches. He had one today and the day before that. He made a mental note to call Dr. Singh in the morning.

Tim leaned back and let his mind trace a path in memory.

Dreamy voices called out, *"Well, what have we here?...That's my dog give her back!...You two look hungry...how about some lunch?...I live right here. I hate eating alone...don't you...my name is Peter what's yours...I'm Tim and this here is my dog, Fate...WOW! This place looks like a church!"*

He roused himself with a groan. Glancing down at Van Wyck Street, he caught a movement that took him back to a September Sunday. The bus from Kensington was heaving its rusty bulk away from the curb blocking the traffic flow on the street.

"They must go to school to learn how to do that," he muttered.

C H A P T E R 44

▼

THREE YEARS LATER

Jan headed for the door with Angela hot on his heels. It was the final movement in a concerto of bitterness they had been rehearsing every night for the past six months. The verbal slugfests had begun on their honeymoon and escalated to oblivion in food and alcohol for Angela and evermore work for Jan.

Interest in sex declined soon after their wedding, his lack of ardor in direct proportion to Angela's ballooning body. All her life Angela had known she was an unwanted child, or at the very least an unexpected addition to her parent's ideal family. Her sister, Elaine, was as beautiful as a film star and as shallow as a mirror. She was reed-thin, and in her parents' eyes that was all that mattered.

In contrast, Angela was as ordinary as a girl could be, the normal kind of person her father disdained as being far too regular for him to notice. Her full figure was the most damning aspect of all. Angela's adoration of her parents did little to mitigate their disappointment. Eating binges alternated with diet fads were only a symptom of a far greater pathology that was now playing itself out in pain and the fear of losing Jan.

After returning to Philadelphia from an extended honeymoon in Europe, they moved into the fashionable Society Hill section of the city. As a boy, Jan only got glimpses of "The Hill" as the crusty Kensington bus skirted the cobbled street that marked the border between the haves and the have-nots. Now at last he had arrived and he did it on his own. He neither asked for nor received help from Tim's private wealth. He worked as an environmental lawyer for one the giant chemical companies lining the Delaware River. The townhouse cost a fortune, but Angela had set her heart on it. So had her mother.

The distraction of decorating her new home lasted just six weeks. Then Angela renewed the sniping. Nothing Jan did satisfied her, and everything he failed to do infuriated her beyond reason. If he was too attentive, he was up to something. If he was cool, he didn't love her. When he zigged, she zagged. There was no end to it and no resolution. Eventually it was Jan who initiated the spats, leaving the house relieved rather than angry, happy to be away from her. But his mock fury didn't fool Angela. She could only guess where he went after their spite-filled brawls.

"This picking a fight every night is nothing but avoidance behavior!" Angela screamed. "You know it's true, Jan Christopher!"

"Just like my mother!" Jan thought. Whenever his mother yelled, she had always called him Jan Christopher.

This evening the words had been especially mean-spirited. Finally they had come to the last barricade. There were no more defenses left to pull down.

"You're right," Jan admitted. "It is avoidance behavior…and more."

"You're sleeping with someone!" she accused.

"Wrong."

"You hate me!"

"Wrong again."

"You're gay."

"Bingo!"

"You son of a bitch! Tim Morris! That's who you've been running off to, isn't it?"

"I haven't spoken to Tim since our wedding day."

"Liar!"

Angela collapsed on the couch sobbing. "You're breaking my heart. Please don't leave me this way."

"I assume you want us to continue to pretend we're happily married until you find someone else."

"Is that so wrong? I think you owe me that much."

"I'm not going to discuss what I owe you. I'm moving to my club. I suggest you find a new fellow soon. Oh, be sure to check him out before you commit. You don't want to get burned again."

"Why do you have to be so mean? I've been good to you," she sobbed.

"No, Angela, you haven't been good to me. You know something? You are unequalled in the art of self-delusion. And like your mother, you're a bully. You need professional help."

Jan counted to ten like Tim did and calmed himself. Sitting beside her, he tried to talk reason.

"Angela, I'm opening the door to a gilded cage. It's a gift, take it."

"Why did you marry me if you're gay?" she cried.

Jan heaved a deep sigh. "As naive as it sounds, I thought it would go away. You know what they say, all a faggot needs is a good taste of pussy to set him straight!"

"You haven't touched my pussy often enough to get straight!"

"Oh yeah? If you weren't so hung up on taste, touch and smell, maybe I would have had a better chance to acquaint myself with it! You dump so much talc down there it's like fucking a jar of glue!"

"You bastard! I hate you!"

"Then we're even. I don't much like myself right now either."

Jan left his wife crying on the couch her mother bought for them without asking if he liked Early American furniture. He left the house Angela's parents picked out for them because, although she was fat and a disappointment, they could at least feel proud of her address. He drove away in the Mercedes sedan Angela's father urged he buy because it went so well with the neighborhood.

For three years, Jan had let himself be corralled, manipulated and browbeaten. He welcomed the abuse because he felt guilty for denying his gayness to everyone, most of all to himself; guilty because he married a girl who wanted, and perhaps deserved, a different kind of life; guilty because he had broken Tim's heart and his promise to carry on the work of Mundus.

Jan drove into Center City pulling into the underground parking lot of the Pinnacle Club. The padded silence of the elevator was comforting. Quiet was what Jan needed right now, that and the nerve to call Tim.

CHAPTER 45

▼

Jan sat all day in the Pinnacle Club's reading lounge working up the courage to walk the few blocks to the Saint Roi and into Tim's arms. Of course, he realized that Tim's arms might be holding someone else. It was a chance he had to take. He was still a member of Mundus and, as such, knew he would be received with courtesy.

The city streets were still wet from a seasonal cloudburst. Jan dodged familiar puddles as he walked up Van Wyck Street. Passing the old flower shop, a sight caught his eye—"Special Today! Large bunch only $10". A voice from the past tugged at his mind. *"My name's Tim. What's yours?"*

Smiling with the memory of that first unsure meeting, Jan sprinted the last few yards and into the serene silence of the Saint Roi. The desk clerk started to challenge him as he passed, but a flash of the gold key card for the thirteenth floor penthouse apartment was enough to ward off the security guard.

The apartment was dark, odd for this time of day. The giant windows that usually gleamed like bright eyes were blind with heavy drapes. At first Jan didn't notice Mrs. Santos sitting in Tim's favorite chair.

"Mrs. Santos?" Jan whispered.

When she didn't answer, Jan knelt beside the chair. "Mrs. Santos," he said louder.

The old lady shuddered. Opening her eyes, she blinked once, twice.

"Mrs. Santos, it's me, Jan."

Jan took her hands in his. He remembered her hands as always being warm and comfortable. Today they were cold.

"*Señor* Jan? Oh, *Señor* Jan!"

She began to weep uncontrollably.

"It's all right, Mrs. Santos. Everything is okay. I'm here."

As he held her to his chest, Jan heard the muffled words, "Too late…too late."

Jan drew back, searching her eyes. "Mrs. Santos, where is Tim?"

"Oh little one, if only you had come sooner," she cried.

"What are you talking about? Where is he?"

"*Muerto.*"

"*Muerto?* Dead? Did you say dead?" Jan asked in disbelief.

Mrs. Santos could only nod her reply.

"No! It can't be true."

Jan tore around the room. "This is a joke. Someone from the lobby called and he knew I was coming so you all are playing a joke."

Jan ran to the bedroom shouting, "Tim!"

Mrs. Santos struggled to her feet and caught him in the in the hall as he returned from the empty bedroom.

"No! *Señor* Jan! Please do not do this!"

Jan put his back against the hall wall and slid to the floor bawling Tim's name. Mrs. Santos rocked him in her arms until he was silent.

They passed an hour in this way, until Jan stirred. "I'm sorry, I must be heavy on you." he murmured.

Mrs. Santos stroked his wet cheek saying, "You have never been heavy on me. Now tell me, what are you doing here? Where is Angela?"

"Ah, Mrs. Santos, Angela and I have split up. I'm filing divorce papers."

"If I may ask, why are you doing this?" she asked.

"Angela was unhappy from the first week of our marriage and it didn't take long for me to realize that I married her to spite Tim for my mother's death and also the way the two of us, umm…the way we were. I was terribly wrong. I came here to ask him to forgive me and to take me back."

Jan wiped his face with the back of his hand.

"I am sorry for you and Angela. I'm sorry for everybody."

"How did he…, I mean, what happened?"

"*Señor* Tim suffered from acute myelogenous leukemia. It strikes adults mostly. He had it a long time but kept it a secret. No one knew until the very last when he was unable to conceal it any longer."

"Why didn't you…, or *somebody* tell me?" Jan demanded angrily.

"He would not permit it. It was the way he wanted it."

Jan put his head on the old woman's shoulder.

"Where is he buried?" Jan asked wearily.

"In France. He wanted to be next to *Señor* Peter."

"Yeah, I can see that."

"Come into the study; there is something for you. I think you will be in for a surprise."

CHAPTER 46

▼

Mrs. Santos led Jan to the desk. She took out three large manila envelopes.

"*Señor* Tim left instructions that if you returned to the Saint Roi within one year after his death you are to receive all his assets. That includes the law practice and the leadership of Mundus in the United States. If after a year you had not returned, Mundus would assemble and select a leader for North America. The law firm was to be sold and the money spread over selected recipients. Since you have returned within the allotted time, these documents are your instructions. The envelope with the blue seal is for Mundus. The one with the red seal is for the Templars of the Law, and the one with the green seal is a personal letter for you. *Señor* Hunter is the executor of the will."

"Thank you," Jan said slipping into the desk chair.

"There is one more thing. You remember Roberto de Silva?" Mrs. Santos said.

"Of course. How is he? Still making beautiful clothes?"

"No. Roberto retired six months ago. He has asked me to marry him. I have accepted his offer. We are to be married in Miami. He has a house there, so I will be leaving."

Jan sat stunned. "But this place can't function without you! *I* can't function here without you!"

"Of course you can. Besides, do you think I would leave without providing for my departure? You remember my daughter, Sonya, no?"

"Certainly."

"She has been working here for several years now and is ready to take over. And it will be better if you have someone closer your own age to look after you."

Jan knew it was no use arguing with this iron-willed woman. Still, he could try to reason.

"What about Mundus and my being gay? Won't those pose problems for her?"

"Sonya knows all about Mundus. She is already a member. She is also aware of your relationship with *Señor* Tim so there will be no issues on homosexuality."

"Thank you for telling me. It does make things a lot easier."

Mrs. Santos left the room quietly as Jan sat at the desk and opened Tim's letter.

My dear Jan,

I see you have returned to the Saint Roi. I can only guess your reasons for doing so and truly hope they have not been painful to you. By now, either Mrs. Santos or Pat Hunter has informed you of the situation and of your great privilege. You should contact Pat for details of my will. It is very straightforward.

I remember saying once that you were embarking on an adventure. I hope I have prepared you well. And Jan, always know that I never stopped loving you. If there is a power from beyond the grave, and I believe there is, I will be beside you always, wherever you may be.

Tim

Jan grieved and wept alone in the gathering gloom. It was close to midnight when he called the Venture Inn to ask Pat if they could meet for lunch and discuss the terms laid out in Tim's will.

"Jan, I don't want to pry, but will Angela be living with you at the Saint Roi? I mean she'll have to know what you're up to in Mundus at some point."

"Look Pat, we've split. Divorce papers are in the works. I'll give you the details another time."

"I understand. We don't have to meet to go over the will. It's all left to you without reservation. I'll get it probated by Jack Hammond. He owes me a favor. By noon tomorrow you'll be cleared to act in Mundus and at the law office. I really don't know if you have the details of Tim's full financial situation but your combined assets now make you one of the top ten wealthiest people in the world. We can let it go at that for now but Tim's accountant will want to go over everything with you sometime in the next few months"

"Thanks Pat. You've always been a good friend. I hope I can count on you in the future. I'll be in touch in a few days."

"Of course, Jan, anytime."

After finishing with Pat, Jan turned their conversation over in his mind. Money. It was poor compensation and it did nothing to lessen his feelings of inadequacy. With Tim by his side, Jan felt that nothing was beyond his reach. Now, everything seemed beyond him.

He called the Pinnacle Club for messages then went into the living room and poured himself a small Campari over ice. He leaned back against the leather-covered wall and rolled the cool crystal glass across his forehead. The spicy aroma brought back memories of Italy, the Gulf of Salerno's sea breeze and the temple of Neptune at Paestum. He was eighteen again, and the world was sweet.

CHAPTER 47

▼

Marsha Betterman met Jan at the Rittenhouse Square entrance to the Templars of the Law. She was the only person in the firm who knew the exact relationship Tim had with Jan.

"Good afternoon, Mr. Phillips. It's nice to see you again. I just wish the circumstances were different."

Jan eyed the woman wondering if she was just being polite or if she really was happy to see him. After all, she was fiercely devoted to Tim and Jan wondered if she could transfer that loyalty to him.

"I've assembled all the staff personnel in the large conference room," Marsha said.

"Thanks. Have you made the payment arrangements for the staff I asked?"

"Yes sir, it's all set," she said.

"Good. Now would you please find out where Hansford Ward is right now? When you do, please get his phone number for me."

Jan went directly to the main conference room, where ninety-three of the world's toughest and smartest lawyers waited to hear if they were still employed. Walls that normally would be paneled or painted held giant plasma screen monitors used for conferencing and case presentation. Clients could, through the magic of technology, communicate visually around the globe. The newest advances in lighting made the space a dream to work in. The long table running almost the length of the room was bare. High-backed leather chairs surrounded the ebony slab. The lone exception was the director's chair. It had been crafted from a two hundred year-old hickory tree that had grown in the center of Rittenhouse Square. The chair was completely unadorned. No arms or padding offered the occupant comfort. It was Tim's way of saying, "I remember where I came from." though no one in the firm had the slightest idea of where that was.

Jan began the meeting. "Good afternoon, everyone."

"Good afternoon, sir," they all chimed.

"This gathering is eating up our clients time so I'll be brief. I expect everyone who has a contract to continue working until it expires. Those of you who have contracts coming due will be asked to stay on another year. I know that due to Tim's illness and death, your pay raises were not authorized for this quarter. You will be relieved to know that when you get back to your desks there will be envelopes with your pay increases and a modest bonus for keeping focused on our clients. If you have questions please address them, in writing, to Marsha. That's all."

As Jan left the room, those closest to him pressed his hands in consolation and gratitude for his generosity.

Marsha followed Jan into Tim's old office. She handed him a slip of paper.

"What's this?"

"It's Mr. Ward's address and phone number. He lives in France now."

Marsha had been beside Jan since the minute he arrived. How could she have gotten this without him noticing?

"Damn your good!" he praised.

"It's what I do. Oh, this is for you. I hope you don't mind. We all chipped in and had it made for your desk."

Marsha handed Jan a long, slim box. Inside he found a silver desk plaque with the motto Tim had given him as a Christmas present those many years ago. *"Do Justice. Love Mercy. Walk Humbly in the Site of Thy God. "*

He shuddered, warding off another burst of tears.

"This is very nice," Jan choked. "Please have thank you notes ready for me to sign later today."

Marsha closed the padded door quietly. Jan placed a call to Paris.

"Han, this is Jan Phillips. I don't know if you've heard, but I'm taking over for Tim."

"Good to hear from you again, Jan. And, yes, I just got a call from Pat Hunter. I'm glad that it's working out this way. Speaking of which, will Angela be on board?"

"Didn't Pat say anything about Angela?"

"No. Should he have?"

"We've split up is all."

"Holy shi…I mean I'm sorry to hear that. Is there anything you need me to do?"

"Actually I wanted to know if Joachim Nusbaum is still active and if so do you think he would join our little band of brothers."

"Nusbaum? Why him?"

"Because he's tough, and I owe him my life. Ask him to meet me in Arles a week from today. You come too, okay?"

"I'll be there."

Jan gently put the phone back in its cradle and thought about Mundus and what course he would take in directing the North American chapter.

Instinct, as well as his training under Tim's careful eye, told him he needed continuity and a clear direction. Decades before the outlined philosophy of the chapter was set down by the first American master. Each succeeding man put his own personal stamp on the office without ever reversing decisions made by the previous occupant of the post. Tim had been very specific about how he envisioned the ideal world. It was up to Jan to make it a reality according to his own lights. For continuity, he needed Hansford Ward, Pat Hunter and Tim's inner circle. For a clear direction he needed new people around him; people his own age and energy. He turned this over in his mind. He prayed he'd be up to the challenge, but Mundus had always carried with it a dark side; a side he drew away from with a combination of fear and fascination.

His thoughts were interrupted when Marsha walked in with the thank you notes. She put them on the desk blotter and turned to leave.

"Marsha, wait," Jan said.

Gesturing to the camelback sofa that faced the large arched window he said, "Would you sit with me a while?"

She studied his face a moment, sensing his need to be with someone who had been close to Tim. She smiled warmly.

"Of course."

They sat in silence, looking down on the hubbub of city life playing out in the confines of the square below.

Finally, Jan drew a deep breath and said, "Marsha, please get me a plane ticket for Arles."

"Do you want the Concorde? She asked.

Jan thought a moment. "No, not this time. This time there's no hurry…, no hurry at all.

END

0-595-30490-7